MW01243475

Scandinavian Secrets - A John Peters Mystery Thriller

By

Robert H. Scott Jr

This book is dedicated to my friends and family who have been so supportive in my writing and in particular this series of novels. Writing is a solitary art and having support from friends and family is important to encourage an author to keep going especially when inspiration wanes.

Introduction

Echo II, the oceanographic ship, rounded the fjord just as the sun was setting and dropped anchor. As winter approached in Norway the sun set later in the day each night. On board, John and Liz Peters were having dinner with Captain James and his wife Angelique. Also at the table was the Peter's son Jack who at age 4 was on his first sea voyage. Fred James was already making a sailor out of him and was telling him of some of their past adventures.

"Jack, the last time we went on an adventure together started out in the Mekong River between Thailand and Laos. One day your mother and father will tell you all about it."

John and Liz smiled knowing that Jack had no idea what Fred was talking about, but he was polite enough to nod his head as though he understood. Jack loved being on the bridge with Fred and being shown all the instruments and controls. Fred had even set up special cushions to raise him up in the Captain's chair and let him work the joystick that controlled the ship. Under his careful eye of course and that of the now Captain of the Echo II, Alfred Hastings. While

Fred owned the Echo II and had captained it for years himself, he had turned over the Captain duties to his first officer Alfred Hastings some years ago.

"John and Liz, you have been pretty secretive about what we are doing in Norway." Fred and Angelique were curious just what they were doing on this trip.

"Actually, Fred we have no idea. Dame Walters called from MI6 headquarters and suggested that we take this trip and plans to meet us in Oslo tomorrow. Knowing her it could be anything. We did ask if it were something that would prevent us from bringing Jack along but she said he would be fine so it cannot be like some of other adventures she has had us involved with." At least that was what John and Liz had hoped.

"What about Harry and Meg and all our other Oxford friends?" Angelique who enjoyed all the friends involved in their two enterprises, the Peters Archaeological Institute and the SAS Securities service run by Harry and Meg Roberts.

"I understood from Dame Walters that they would likely be joining us at the end of the week. Just what she has in mind I have no idea. But from our past experiences it should prove interesting if M of MI6 is involved.

"We can take the tender into town tonight if you want or we can wait until tomorrow when we dock in Oslo." Fred mentioned but it was agreed they would enjoy just being at anchor for the evening.

Later that night both couples were sitting on the afterdeck enjoying the light display of the Northern Lights. A sight for those given the privilege of seeing it was not to be missed. Jack was mesmerized by the display which was like a fireworks display for him. It was hoped that the meeting with Dame Walters later in the week would be equally illuminating.

Chapter One

The next morning at breakfast Liz and John were discussing with Fred James and Angelique their past adventures and experiences with Dame Walters, the M of MI6 and Clark Rathbone, the Director of the CIA.

"In light of our experience I doubt that Dame Walters has invited us here for a social visit much as we enjoy seeing her and Clark. But I also cannot believe she would put Jack at risk having him along."

"I agree. Our time looking for Alexander's tomb (Operation Black Amphora) certainly would have put Jack at danger. Same with our stopping a virus spread by cruise ships (The Devil's Dagger) not to mention the attempt to melt the polar ice cap (Treasures of the Deep). At least we have not been involved in anything dangerous since our time in Thailand and off China stopping an EMP weapon to be developed that could have thrown us back to the early 19th Century without any modern technology (Mystery on the Mekong)." John and Liz had spent a good part of the night wondering what Dame Walters wanted them to be involved with this time.

Fred James and Angelique were two of the Peters best friends with Fred having been involved in all the past adventures and Angelique having met and married Fred when they were in Arles, France searching for the Arles Wreck and ending up preventing a melting of the polar ice cap.

"Will be good to have everyone together again next week if this all works out." Angelique had become fond of all the group of adventurers that seemed to grow with each new adventure. At the core of the group in addition to John and Liz Peters were Harry and Meg Roberts. Harry who had been part of SAS and then MI6 and Meg who had been a scientist working with DARPA, the US Defense agency tasked with creating new inventions for the DOD and now working with the British equivalent. They were also running SAS Security Services out of Oxford where John and Liz had their Archaeological Institute as part of St. Edmunds Hall, one of the Oxford University smaller but historic colleges.

"I assume that Sally and Martin will be joining us too?" Angelique asked.

"Yes, Sally is just finishing up teaching her class and doing bit of research and Martin is wrapping up that last security assignment." Martin Fredricks and wife Sally had been involved since the polar ice cap adventure. Martin retired from the Navy had served with Fred James in the Navy and now had been recruited to Oxford along with his wife who, with her Ph.D., was a virus specialist.

"What are Maria and Nicos up to by the way" Fred asked John and Liz.

"They are just back from Mexico spending time in Belize doing some diving and seeing if there is anything left from the cave where the Devil's Dagger was first found. They even took their daughter along to see her grandfather in Mexico City. I am sure he has had a grand time showing her around the museum he heads. But they are to be back in Oxford in a couple of days."

Maria from Mexico and Nicos from Crete had been involved in the Devils Dagger business and since then had both been working with John and Liz and teaching at Oxford. They planned to leave their daughter with her mother in London when they left to join Echo II in Norway.

Harry and Meg had a new son, Randy, who was same age as Jack, John and Liz's son and Athena, Maria and Nicos daughter. At the time of the EMP adventure in the Mekong and the South China Sea all three women, Liz, Meg and Maria had been pregnant. Angelique was so glad she was past all of that. But she was honorary grandmother to all three and loved having them on board Echo II. She was

disappointed all three would not be joining them but was glad both Jack and Randy would be coming along with them.

"And what about Ming Lee?" Fred asked Meg.

"She is in London working on that EMP device making sure that they understand how serious that could be if it ever were used. It would make the atomic bomb look like a cap pistol in terms of the damage it would do to society."

Ming Lee had been an interpreter in the Mekong adventure. She turned out to be a graduate engineer with many skills and while she was an agent with MI6 in Thailand Dame Walters had agree do let her join with the Oxford group, as they were staring to be known, while still working with MI6 from time to time. She had recently completed her Ph.D. which Sally Fredricks had encouraged her to do and would be teaching next year at St. Edmunds. They were thrilled to have two women professors of the stature of Ming Lee and Sally Fredricks not to mention John and Liz Peters. But with their involvement in projects that MI6 and the CIA kept getting them involved with their teaching would more than occasionally take a back seat.

"I understand that Ming is already in Oslo and will be meeting us today and then coming on board Echo II. Dame Walters says that she has been doing great work in London with Meg on the EMP project."

Fred chuckled and Angelique asked him what was so funny.

"You do know that Ming Lee and Harold have been dating?" Harold was the technology wizard on board the Echo II who had been working with Meg on all their technology gadgets but since Ming Lee came into the picture had been spending more and more time with her.

"No, I did not know that!" Angelique smiled thinking that Ming Lee and Harold had a lot in common and it would be nice for Harold to be even more involved than he has been.

"Yes, in fact he even asked if there might be a place for him in Oxford after this trip and I told him I thought that could be worked out. He could be especially useful in the SAS Security operation, but I think his interest is being closer to Ming Lee than to working with SAS." Fred was smiling too as Harold had been with him for a long time; but he also wondered how Ming Lee's upscale Chinese parents living in Australia now having moved from Hong Kong years ago would take to the red-haired Scotsman, Harold McDougal. That could prove an interesting family visit Fred was thinking.

But that is getting ahead of things as they had only started dating this last year although it did seem their relationship was blossoming, and Meg had been encouraging it as she had taken Harold under her wing.

"All I know is that it will be nice to have everyone together again. Seems like as time passes, we are like ships passing in the night these days. But at least we all have our base in Oxford." Fred commented.

It was mid-morning before they up upped the anchor and docked in Oslo just in time to leave for the MI6 offices to meet with Dame Walters and find out what she was up to.

They decided to walk from the port of Christiania to the MI6 offices which were nearby. They wanted to enjoy some of the sights as the day was beautiful, if brisk. Seeing the friendly Norwegians, they nodded to along the way it reminded them of what they went through with German occupation during WWII.

Fred James commented that the Germans treated Norway hugely different from Denmark, at least in the beginning and up to 1943 when atrocities became pronounced in Denmark as well as Norway. Denmark capitulated quickly and negotiated as best they could with Germany. As a result, they were treated far more leniently to start with than the Norwegians who resisted and even sunk one of the German cruisers in the Oslo harbor. The resistance in Norway was treated in the early days much more harshly; especially when compared to Denmark. And the Danes were as a result able to smuggle most of their Jewish population to safety in Sweden throughout the early part of the war.

While in Oslo, with the nice weather, they were hoping to spend some time taking Jack and the other kids to see some of the sights. At age four they would not remember much but it was always fun to see how excited they get seeing new things. They knew that Fred and Angelique were champing at the bit to take Jack and Randy to show them all a good time. As for John and Liz they wanted to enjoy some of the smorgasbord that let them try a lot of local cuisine. They had not been to Scandinavia in a while so were hoping to make a bit of a vacation out of the trip.

Among the sites they wanted to see was the Akershus Castle and Fortress dating from the 1300's. They knew it had a great view of the city and they could get oriented to other sites to enjoy while in Oslo. Since the rest of the Oxford Group, as they were starting to be called by Dame Walters, would not be joining them for a few days surely there would be time to enjoy one of the more remarkable Scandinavian capitals.

As for the adults they wanted to see the Norwegian Opera and Ballet building which was a remarkable piece of architecture. Not quite as stunning as the Sydney Opera House they had visited last year it was nevertheless a remarkable edifice in white marble and its unique architecture. Sloped like a ski slope, which seemed appropriate for Norway, with masses of glass it was light and airy. Sloping to the water it seemed almost like a ship ready to leave dry dock. They had a view of it from the Echo II as they entered the harbor and could not wait for a visit to the building itself.

Also, on the agenda that Liz and Angelique were working up was the Munch museum with the works of the artist Edvard Munch, his most famous work perhaps being The Scream which is in the

National Museum and while not on display until 2022 it will be then on display in a special room devoted to his art. While not a great favorite artist of theirs it would be like visiting Amsterdam and not taking in the Rembrandt or Van Gogh museums.

They knew a big hit with Jack and with Fred and Martin too would be the Viking Ship Museum with its fully reconstructed Viking ship. The museum had the best collection of preserved Viking ships anywhere in the world. John and Liz had already contacted the curator who was anxious to show them the museum and discuss the latest finds of Viking material. He also wanted to discuss the dig that John and Liz had discussed doing in the region in conjunction with the museum and the local university.

For the moment sightseeing had to be put on hold until they knew what Dame Walters wanted. Fortunately, the walk from Echo II to the MI6 office took them to Huk Avenue where the ship museum was located. John and Liz stopped in for a minute to say hello and set up a meeting on Echo II with the curator for the evening.

Jars Svenson, the curator, was more than happy to agree to a dinner on the Echo II hoping to encourage the exploration of a new potential

Viking site in the north of Norway near Tromso. Knowing that their children would be there he planned to bring along a Viking horned hat for Jack and Randy which he knew would be a big hit with the kids as his nephews had fun with theirs.

As a curator always on the hunt for more artifacts for his museum he was not beyond small bribes like this to encourage parents to add donations to his collection. But in this case, he genuinely cared about John and Liz having worked with them before and he knew no encouragement was really needed. Still, it never hurt to pamper children of prospective donors.

The offices of MI6 were in the Norwegian Trading Company building which, of course, was nothing of the sort. Trading that went on here was information and not products. After passing security and given their visitor badges, they were taken to the conference room where they found Dame Walters and Ming Lee waiting for them along with Harold McDougal.

The first fifteen minutes were spent talking with Ming Lee about her trip and catching up while having coffee and chatting. Dame Walters observed her friends and thought to herself how lucky they all were to be able to work together. Not often that M of MI6 found herself among friends she really enjoyed and could let her hair down as she could not do within MI6. But she had to remind herself this was also a business meeting.

"I hope all are enjoying this new Norwegian coffee I found at the coffee shop around the corner, but it is time I brought you up to date on why we are here. I have already told Ming Lee and Harold but now it is time to let you know why I asked you here to Norway."

Seeing she had their attention she continued, "We have had reports from the scientists at the University of Bergan that concern us. It appears that there has been a significant change in the pattern of the Northern Lights. As you know this is a factor of radiation from the sun interacting with our upper atmosphere. You probably saw some of the effects last night?" She saw everyone nod as they had spent the evening enjoying the light display but did not realize how unusual it apparently was to see this in Oslo.

"It is not unusual to see the Northern Lights in this latitude, but the length and extent of the display has increased rather dramatically in recent weeks and they are at a loss to explain the phenomenon."

Dame Walters let this sink in but then suggested that Harold comment as he had already, with Ming Lee, been meeting with the scientists who were in Oslo visiting with colleagues.

"We met with the scientists yesterday afternoon and while they are not alarmed yet at what they are seeing they just cannot explain why we are seeing such intense Northern Lights as there is no radiation increase from the sun to explain it. Looking over all the history of studying the Northern Lights there has never been another event like this."

John stepped into the conversation at this point. "Is there a concern here or just a mystery as to why this is happening?" He was having trouble seeing why Dame Walters had them involved with what seemed a scientific problem.

"To be honest, they really don't know. The good news is that the event has increased tourism to Norway exponentially. Which is good as tourism dried up during the Covid crisis. Tour boats are taking people away from city lights to see the spectacular display. Hotels are filled to capacity and airlines are having trouble keeping up with people wanting to see this while it lasts. Usually, it is a matter of luck to get to see Northern Lights but right now you can count on a display every night."

"So that is a good thing." Liz injected.

"Yes, for now, but the scientists are concerned that without an explanation for what is causing this to happen there might be a dark side to what is happening. They are frank about it that they just do not know."

Dame Walters took over again. "We have asked the key scientists to meet with us tonight on the Echo II if that is ok with everyone and let them explain."

Fred James commented that this was fine, but John pointed out they had invited Lars Svenson to have dinner with them tonight and wondered if that would be a problem.

"No actually he has been involved with this already as some of the most intense activity has been seen from his recent expedition and Viking site on the northern coast of Norway. So, having him with us tonight is a plus and I was actually going to suggest it."

Liz nudged John and her eyes told him to look at Ming Lee and Harold. He smiled with Liz and he saw the two of them acting bit like teenagers which for two scientists of their stature was bit funny but also rather cute. It was increasingly obvious that their dating was leading to much more and they hoped that Ming Lee's conservative Chinese background was not going to be a problem for the couple. Same of course for Harold's Scottish parents. They learned last week that the two had taken an apartment together in Oxford.

The meeting broke up with John and Liz going back to the Viking Museum to spend time with Lars and discuss what he knew about the Northern Lights phenomenon as well as their project they were considering working on together. Fred and Angelique along with Harold and Ming Lee headed back to the Echo II.

When John and Liz arrived back at Echo II after bit of sightseeing, they were pleased to see that Harry and Meg had arrived with their young son Randy who was busy playing with Jack on the back deck. The crew had built a play fort for the young boys and even at four years old they were having a grand time exploring the fortress.

In the quarters that Fred and Angelique kept for themselves on Echo II, which was Fred's private yacht having given over Captain duties years ago now to his first officer, they were enjoying spending time catching up with Harry and Meg. It was on the cruise where Fred and Angelique met doing a search in Arles France that his friends learned that Fred was in face a British Earl and immensely wealthy, something he had kept quiet about in their earlier adventures. Since then, all had come to terms with this change in status for Fred and all had been overjoyed when he and Angelique were married.

"That is really strange that Dame Walters has us all involved in this Northern Lights business." Harry was genuinely puzzled.

"I am happy that we are all together again and I must admit I have never seen the Northern Lights, so I am excited to see this tonight." Meg added as neither of them had seen this light display.

"We will have several guests tonight, Lars Svenson curator of the Viking Museum and two scientists from the University of Bergen, Drs Peterson, husband and wife team, Freda and Hans. So, I thought we would leave the dock tonight around 6 and after dinner we will be out at sea away from city lights to really get to see the lights."

"It will be interesting to see Jack and Randy when they see this as it is almost like a fireworks display from what I have heard." Meg and Harry were obviously excited to see the lights. "Yes, we saw them last night while at anchor, but the city lights did interfere a bit so being away from the city should be even more spectacular." Liz added.

"And it will give Freda and Hans a chance to explain to us why this is significant and just why Dame Walters wants us involved. There has to be more to this than just the scientific curiosity." Fred added what everyone was thinking.

Talk then turned to what was happening in Oxford and the new projects that Harry and Meg were working on with SAS Security Services, the company in which all those in the Oxford group were involved including Fred James and Martin Fredricks. And just as they were enjoying a second coffee there was a hail from the dock asking permission to come aboard. It was Martin and Sally Fredricks who has just arrived in Oslo. So, it appeared that the entire Oxford group was now assembled. Maria and Nicos had arrived a bit earlier but were off exploring the city. Angelique was sorry that they did not bring their daughter, Athena, along but Maria had told her that her mother in London insisted on a visit but that she had agreed to bring Athena to Oslo in a day or two to join them having learned of the Northern Lights display and wanting to see them herself and allow Athena to see them.

Angelique was looking forward to having all three of the four-year-old children on board and had plans to spoil them all while they were here. The crew of Echo II looked forward to their visits and the only problem was who among the crew would be allowed to babysit.

"Well at least on this trip it seems we have a curiosity to explore but nothing like the dangers we have faced in the past. I cannot imagine Dame Walters getting the kids exposed to anything dangerous, so it is possible this trip is more a pleasure trip." Fred commented, but he was also thinking that he knew better.

M of MI6 was a good friend, but she would not be wasting her or their time on this issue if there were not something more involved. But as a god parent to two of the children he knew Dame Walters would not expose them to risk. And if they did run into problems, they could be left in Oslo he supposed. In fact, the three would likely have a wonderful time exploring Oslo once they tired of shipboard life. Then again, they seldom tired of enjoying life on Echo II and were always pleading with their parents to go back on board. As much as the crew spoiled them, he could understand why. But hopefully whatever the problem Dame Walters wanted to involve them in surely it could not be that serious.

Chapter Two

The sun was starting to set when everyone was on board for the evening dinner and cruise. They crew was casting off the dock lines and Captain Hastings was preparing to head out to sea in time for watching the evening Northern Lights display. By the time dinner was over dark should be complete and the show ready to begin.

Dinner was a lively event with everyone getting acquainted with the curator of the Viking Museum as well as the two scientists from the University of Bergen who were sharing the sites that must be seen while in Norway. They also knew of the past adventures and had many questions especially for Ming Lee, Meg and Harold about the technology on the Echo II. Fortunately, Ming Lee and Meg were of the same age as the Petersons and seemed they had much in common in their scientific interests.

Before leaving the dinner, the talk turned of more serious matters. Dame Walters opened the discussion asking if Freda would explain the concerns, she and her husband had that resulted in the Norwegian government asking for Britain to be of help.

"We have noticed that the Northern Lights have changed this year. Rather dramatically in fact. Most of the time you would see the Northern Lights only when there was increased radiation coming from the sun that reacts with our atmosphere. While we see the lights frequently, not nearly as much as this year. And not with the intensity. Of course, our tourist bureau is thrilled as it has increased our tourist business which was badly hurt by the Covid crisis and was only now starting to recover."

"What is it that concerns you that you would be asking for our help?" Harold spoke up which was unusual for him as he usually let Meg speak for the team on technology. But ever since he and Ming Lee began to be a couple, he had been much more confident and outspoken. Fred shared a wink with Angelique as they were pleased to see him show more confidence.

"We were not concerned to start with. Things happen from time to time that cannot be explained but as this has gone on and there is no scientific reason for it, we have become concerned there might be something more involved. Either some phenomenon we know nothing about or perhaps something going on that is man made on earth that is somehow involved. Climate change has been raised as possibility whether man made or an earth cycle or some combination. But we are at a loss to understand the change which is why we reached out to our government and they in turn got in touch with your government."

"We are certainly glad to help if we can but frankly we are puzzled why MI6 involvement." Harry spoke up as he was finding this strange.

Dame Walters answered Harry's question. She said that consulting with her scientific board they felt that Meg had done such good work with them that they felt she and her team would be good to investigate the problem. Also, there was concern that the Chinese had been increasing their activity in the North Sea in recent months and while it is unlikely they are involved considering their past activities, with which everyone here on the British side had been involved, it seemed wise to include them in seeking an answer.

At this point Jars added his thoughts. "The project that John and Liz have been working on with us is in the very north part of Norway. We have been seeing teams of Chinese visiting this area recently which has struck us as odd as they have no business interests in the area nor have they seemed to have any interest in the work we are doing. They are clearly not tourists. It may have nothing to do with what else they might be doing or with the Northern Lights issue, but I thought it worth mentioning."

The discussion continued for some time, but no conclusions were reached. In the end it was decided they would give this some thought as to how best to proceed and for now just go on deck to watch the light show.

The light show was truly incredible and was far more brilliant than they had seen before and lasted much longer into the night. Freda pointed out that typically you could not count on seeing the Northern Lights and especially this far south in Norway. Normally you would want to go as far north as possible and stay for a long period of time if you hoped to see them. That was what is making this so strange. Wonderful for tourism but troubling for scientists. At least until they can come up with an explanation.

"We hope there is a credible scientific explanation for what we are seeing and that people can continue to enjoy the light show but at the same time just as with changes in climate we worry that there is something we are missing, something that might not be so enjoyable as the light show."

"What analysis have you done to try and explain what is happening?' Meg and Ming Lee asked at the same time.

"We have studied all the past northern light events and can explain them with activity on the sun and its interaction with our atmosphere. The relationship is quite simple and direct although the effects vary. But this time there is no explanation of solar activity which is why this so puzzling."

"We know there was a problem with the ozone layer and release of chlorofluorocarbons (CFC's) which have been universally banned and the ban seems to have worked to start to repair the ozone layer. Is it possible something like this is occurring that could affect the atmosphere and its reaction to normal solar radiation reaching the upper atmosphere" Ming Lee was trying to think of possibilities.

"That is one concern. With the reduction in ozone harming gasses there have been signs of repair to the ozone layer and the hole that was discovered over Antarctica, but that is the very reason we are so concerned with what is happening with the Northern Lights." Freda continued to speak for she and her husband although Hans would occasionally add a thought.

"We have tried to see if there is some explanation in terms of gasses that are affecting the upper atmosphere but so far we have found nothing that provides an answer." Hans added to what Freda had mentioned. He then went on to explain some basics of the aurora borealis or Northern Lights.

"When solar storms send particles to earth those particles interact with our magnetic field and excite the electrons causing them to give off light. A similar phenomenon occurs on earth in neon lights where electricity is used to excite atoms causing brilliant lights in tube."

Hans continued to explain. "One reason we are concerned now is we are also detecting slight changes in the magnetic field at the north pole and in the northern regions of Norway too. While it is not at all unusual to see minor changes in the magnetic field these changes seem to be happening at the same time we are seeing these changes in the Northern Lights making us wonder if there is not some common cause. If so and there is risk to the magnetic field this becomes a potential for a global disaster." Hans let everyone absorb the possible implications.

Meg spoke up adding that she and DARPA (the Defense Advance Research Projects Agency) in the United States and the British equivalent with which she now as working had been concerned about the changes in the magnetic field.

"We know that there has been a reverse of the polar fields numerous times in the earth's history and that the last one was some 780,000 years ago. Sometimes this happens as frequently as 20,000 years and sometimes not for millions of years. But when there are significant changes in the field the risk that a reversal of the magnetic field may be occurring is a concern that cannot be ignored. When this happens the north and south poles reverse. North America then becomes South America. At least so far as the polar relationship is concerned. Compasses which pointed to the north pole now point not north but south." Meg continued to explain.

"There is a relationship between the earth's magnetic field and the lights plus the different colors depends on the elements being excited by the solar radiation. NASA has commented on this and this is what they have had to say." Hans pulled up on the large computer screen the information from NASA so all could see.

He went on to cite from the NASA discussion that it has been known for some time that the lights are caused by reactions between the high-energy particles of solar flares colliding in the upper regions of our atmosphere and then descending along the lines of the planet's magnetic fields. Green lights tell of oxygen being struck at a certain altitude, red or blue of nitrogen.

"But the patterns — sometimes broad, sometimes spectral, sometimes curled and sometimes columnar — are the result of the magnetic field that surrounds the planet. The energy travels along the many lines of that field, and lights them up to make our magnetic blanket visible. Such a protective magnetic field is viewed as essential for life on a planet, be it in our solar system or beyond."

https://astrobiology.nasa.gov/news/the-northern-lights-the-magnetic-field-and-life/

Freda continued, noting that in the same article NASA goes on to point out how important the magnetic field is to life on the planet and its interaction with the Northern Lights can be indicative of major changes that threaten the planet. She pointed out the following from NASA:

"In these collisions, the energy of the electrons is transferred to the oxygen and nitrogen and other elements in the atmosphere, in the process exciting the atoms and molecules to higher energy states. When they relax back down to lower energy states, they release their energy in the form of light. This is like how a neon light works. The aurora typically forms 60 to 400 miles above Earth's surface."

"All this is possible because of our magnetic field, which scientists theorize was created and is sustained by interactions between super-hot liquid iron in the outer core of the Earth's center and the rotation of the planet. The flowing or convection of liquid metal generates electric currents, and the rotation of Earth causes these electric currents to form a magnetic field which extends around the planet."

"If the magnetic field were not present those highly charged particles coming from the sun, the ones that set into motion the processes that produce the Northern and Southern Lights, would instead gradually strip the atmosphere of the molecules needed for life." Freda let this last part of the NASA analysis stay on the screen.

"So, are we seeing the same thing happening with the Southern Lights?" Meg asked.

"Yes, we have been in touch with scientists in both Chili and Argentina and they are seeing the

same thing happening in the southern hemisphere."
Hans added.

As the discussion went on it was theorized
that the changes in the Northern and Southern
Lights might have to do with the changes in the
earth's magnetic field more than some event on the
Sun.   But what was happening and more
importantly why was the big question yet to be
answered.

Dame Walters stepped into the conversation
at this point adding that her concern and that of the
CIA was that if there are significant changes in the
magnetic field occurring it could cause all kinds of
problems   for   the   advanced   nations   from
interference with satellites to major medical issues
and perhaps even vast changes in ability to sustain
life in parts of the planet if not the entire planet.

"In light of the efforts by the Chinese CPC
to interfere with the planet for their economic and
political advantage we cannot rule out their
involvement.   Just how or why they would be
messing with the magnetic field is something we
do not know.   But their presence in Norway and
the area around Norway when this is happening
certainly raises eyebrows." Dame Walters let that
sink in as it now appeared that what is happening
might be far more dangerous than anyone on board
had thought up to now.

"I wonder if we should not send Jack and Randy back to England." Liz raised the question as she and Meg caught each other's eyes and knew they were both thinking the same thing.

Dame Walters said that she agreed. That things had changed from when she first got involved. At first, she thought this was purely a scientific expedition and one that the children would enjoy being part of. But if there is Chinese involvement they all knew this could turn dangerous and nasty. It was agreed that Harry would take the children back to England tomorrow and arrange for the grandparents to take care of them while the investigation in Norway continued. It would only take him a short time to get to England and back and he could rejoin the Echo II in a couple of days at most. He was already on the phone to the grandparents making arrangements. They, of course, would be more than happy to have the boys for a visit.

Everyone knew that they were disappointed not to have Jack and Randy on the cruise but keeping them safe was the priority. They would both be disappointed but at least they had a couple of days to enjoy the trip and if it turned out that there was not a danger to them they could always be brought back aboard. Fred and Angelique were particularly disappointed, but they also agreed this was the right decision.

While the concern over the cause was now clear they were still enjoying the light show that was so bright outside the city lights. Everyone brought jackets with them along with heavy sweaters underneath as the night was as cold as it was clear. The display was remarkable tonight. Dancing across the sky and changing colors and shapes it was like viewing a kaleidoscope but in real life and on a giant scale.

Meg was explaining to the boys what they were seeing and, while young as they were they would not really understand, it was a sight they hoped they would remember for a lifetime. While different from a fireworks display it was in many ways far more impressive as the lights danced from horizon to horizon and covered the entire sky.

John and Liz who had seen the Northern and Southern Lights before noted just how much more spectacular was this display. The colors were more vivid and seemed to dance across the sky far more than the previous times they had seen them. Beautiful and awe inspiring but also troubling knowing that this could be something sinister as well as beautiful.

"Meg am I wrong, or did not Tesla do research into electricity claiming that he could provide unlimited electrical energy by manipulating the earth's inherent electrical properties?" Harry asked, trying to remember what he knew of Tesla the genius who is less remembered than his counterpart Edison but who was responsible for creating AC current and the Westinghouse corporation. Despite his mental issues late in life his contributions to science in the form of AC current, radio transmission and induction motors was amazing. And he had far greater potential this Serbian immigrant to the United States.

"Yes, he thought he could provide free electricity though a wireless power grid. In fact, he tested his theory on Pikes Peak in Colorado and proved that he could light a bulb wirelessly. But unfortunately, a combination of forces opposed him, and he was never able to develop the concept. But J.P. Morgan was intrigued and financed the building of the Wardenclyffe tower in New York which was a high-power magnifying tower at first intended to transmit radio waves until Marconi beat him to transmission across the Atlantic. He then turned to using the tower for transmission of electrical energy. His idea was to permit tapping into energy from the earth with anyone being able to use this free energy. Unfortunately, Morgan was threatened in his financial interests by this development and stopped funding."

"Do I recall that there is a massive Tesla tower in Russia still to this day?" Harry asked Meg.

"Yes, and there is little known about it. The Russians are very secretive. It is located about 40 miles outside of Moscow. But supposedly while it could create enough energy to power the entire country for a millisecond the cost of operating the tower caused it to be shut down. Still, it is intriguing." Meg had been studying Tesla for some time now and was intrigued by the concepts he was testing but unfortunately never had the financing to complete. And most scientists dismissed his ideas as not based on good science. Still ideas often dismissed in one generation turn out later to have some validity.

"Is it possible that the Chinese are making use of Tesla like devices to interfere with the ionosphere perhaps also the earth's magnetic field and this could explain what we are seeing?" Freda asked Meg.

"That is certainly something to consider. I would not put it past them. They do not seem to have the same moral or ethical restraints that control science in the Western world. Our past experience with them has shown them to be less than responsible when it comes to their scientific endeavors." Meg remembered their attempt to melt the polar ice cap and to develop an EMP device that could throw the world back two hundred years or more.

"One thing to consider is that we have thwarted several of their efforts over the years so I would not be surprised if they are constantly watching our activities. So, we must move cautiously while we investigate. Freda and Hans, you could be in danger along with the rest of us. Jars that includes you as well. We must assume that the Chinese have their spies in your universities as well as ours and those in the United States and they will be paying attention to what we are doing. So, we should discuss how we can disguise what we are doing to throw them off what we are really up to." Harry saw immediately that this had gone from a pleasure trip into something far more dangerous than any of them had thought.

John spoke up at this point. "Harry, I think we should work with Jars and appear to be doing nothing more than following up on the archaeological dig up north. Depending on what they are up to we may not fool them, but they might at least wait to see what we are doing before they consider taking action against us."

Discussion turned to whether to keep Jack and Randy part of the trip which might help to fool the Chinese but in the end it was decided that the risk was just too great. Dame Walters was on the phone arranging for her jet to take her back to England. While Harry had planned to take the children back himself, she agreed to do this for him thinking it was important for Harry and his SAS personnel on Echo II to stay in Norway to protect the expedition. She would make sure they got to their grandparents safely.

The handling of the children decided it was next decided that Ming Lee and Harold would work with Freda and Hans at their university doing research before joining the rest of the group in northern Norway. It was also agreed that they would continue to so some sightseeing around Oslo again with the hope that it might fool the Chinese. But after their last adventure in the Pacific where they did sightseeing in Hong Kong and Taiwan it was doubted this would fool them for long, if at all.

The night having turned even colder they returned to the lounge for a nightcap before turning in and heaving back to Oslo. While it had been exciting to see the display of Northern Lights that excitement was tempered by knowledge that something was happening that could cause serious damage to the planet. And if it were man made then stopping whatever was going on had to be a top priority.

Chapter Three

Far to the north in Tromso, Norway there was a meeting of the Chinese working group. Tromso is far north in Norway nearly to the top of the country and far within the Artic Circle. North of Iceland it is where Northern Lights tourists flocked to see the Northern Lights before the current displays which now could be seen at bit warmer climates to the south. Still, this was a primary place for study and seeing the light display. But that was not the interest of the group assembled tonight.

"Our students at the University of Bergen report that two professors have raised questions about the Northern Lights displays and have reached out to MI6 and that same group from Oxford that caused us so much trouble before. It seems that they are now in Norway so we must be careful to keep appearances as innocent as possible. We are taking steps to try to discredit the two professors and using social media to disparage them as rouge scientists. We are also using our hackers to try and disrupt their work at the university." Wang Po the lead supervisor on Project Polar was speaking to his scientists who had been flown in from the drilling platform in the North Sea.

"Having students and our propaganda arms active on campuses around the world is paying big dividends. The same is true of our Confucius Institutes which supposedly spread our culture but in fact are designed for promoting the aims of the CPC. Our principal propaganda arm on university campuses. And by giving grants to schools and selected professors we assure that we are welcome and preventing anyone from interfering with our ultimate aims."

Wang Po continued, " We not only can obtain new technology without having to spend to create the technology but can make sure that we derail any activities we do not agree with, sowing discord and distrust. By opening the doors to companies for both manufacturing and to sell products we have made sure that they will not oppose us. The same is true of politicians who we have coopted by creating business opportunities for their family members which will disappear if they do not do our bidding. We will not have to win a war to dominate the world if this strategy continues to work as brilliantly as it has in recent years."

Wang Po noted that all those in attendance were nodding in agreement. They had been carefully selected to be the strongest believers in the CPC vision of the future. As always, he was studying those selected to make sure there was no deviation from their plan. Already two team members who had appeared to be weakening had been returned to China and quietly eliminated.

"For now, we must appear to be merely an innocent scientific mission combined with a business searching for mineral deposits to exploit for the benefit of both Norway and China. Let them investigate all they want. We are patient and once they fail to find anything out of the ordinary, we can continue our real work."

"For how long will we be down?" The drill rig supervisor asked.

" I cannot imagine they will spend more than a few weeks, if that long, following up on the alarms of the scientists as we have stopped for now our activation of Project Polar. As you know the entire design is calculated to be on and offline periodically as that is what will achieve our ultimate objective. So, for now we are offline."

"Perhaps this would be a good time to give our workers some rest and relaxation?"

"No, I want no one leaving the drill rig without my express permission. We cannot take the risk of someone saying or doing something that will alert the authorities." Wang Po made it clear by the looks he gave the five men that his orders would be carried out without question.

"When will the new equipment be delivered?" The lead engineer asked. He had been expecting the new equipment for some time.

"I am assured that it will be here this week and I want it stored locally in the warehouse for now and not transmitted to either the archaeological site or the drill rig. Were the authorities to see this equipment it would be clear to them we are not just engaged in scientific inquiry." The warehouse located in Oslo would need added security and Wang Po made a note to increase its security before the equipment arrived.

The meeting had been held on the tender from the drill rig. Before the meeting ended Wang Po made sure that each of those attending understood that he would expect blind obedience and the alternative hardly had to be explained. They had already lost two of their team who after return to China had not been heard from. All knew what that meant.

Wang Po felt it was a shame, but that tender would never make it back to the drill rig. While he had faith in the men at the meeting, he had been instructed by Beijing to eliminate all those who had detailed knowledge of their project. He wondered if ultimately that would include himself as well but at least for now it was only the supervisor and engineers on the drill rig. While on board he had planted the explosive and set the timer. They would disappear without a trace in another hour. He had made that certain.

Engineers were easy to obtain, and secrecy was the highest priority to the CPC. Already he had made a request of the Ministry that they send a new crew along with the new equipment. The crew would be kept in Oslo for now until it was time to reactivate the Polar Project.

Wang Po thought it was now time for him to meet with the two Dr. Petersons as director of the Chinese scientific expedition and make sure that he could lead them to the conclusion that he wanted and make sure that they had no knowledge of the ultimate objective. If there was any doubt, then it was simple enough to arrange a convenient accident. But he did not think that would be necessary. After all he had arranged for them to secure a large grant for their research from his Ministry in China. The threat of disclosing the source, of which they were unaware, would discredit them and likely lead to prosecution in Norway. He was sure they would not be a problem.

On his way to the airport to fly from Tromso to Oslo he received the sad news that the tender had suffered an explosion on board and all souls lost. He immediately transmitted the preplanned press release to his office in Oslo to be sent in the morning to the various news services expressing the deep sense of loss at the tragedy. He really was saddened that he had been ordered to carry out the killings especially as he felt that there was no risk of disclosure by men he had personally selected. But he also knew enough not to object when told what he was to do. You only objected once and if you did so you immediately because the problem to be eliminated.

In Oslo the next morning Wang Po arranged for a helicopter to take him to the University of Bergan where he was to meet with Freda and Hans Peterson. With him were the two oceanographers that China had provided to him giving cover to the scientific aspects of the project. Likewise, two geologists also provided for the same purpose. The five of them would meet with the Petersons to discuss the projects they were working on together. Wang Po had developed genuine affection for the Petersons and hoped that they would never come under scrutiny from Beijing requiring them to also be dealt with. He knew that should that happen he had no alternative but to obey the order. Not only was he at risk but his family in China as well.

The rewards for his success were substantial but the penalty for failure was something he could not even think about. He had long gone past the point of no return with this project.

The trip by road from Oslo to Bergen or the train would take at least eight hours, so he had decided to take the helicopter for the trip. This would give him time with the oceanographers and geologists to be sure that they understood the next steps in the plan. While noisy it would also be private as the pilots were from the Chinese military and knew better than to listen to his conversation. Not that the scientists with him knew about the real plan only their small part in creating a subterfuge of a scientific investigation.

The trip over to Bergen would give him time to make sure the cover story was fully understood by the men and he had already arranged a flight back to Oslo once the meeting in the early afternoon was concluded. The four scientists with him would remain in Bergen to work with and monitor the activities of the Petersons. He assumed the Petersons would be going to Tromso with the group on the Echo II. At least he thought it likely that was where they would be going. He would know later today after the meeting.

On the way he enjoyed the rugged countryside below as they passed through the mountain range still snowcapped that separated Bergen from Oslo. He was contemplating changing his plans and taking the train back to Oslo as it was one of the more spectacular train trips in all of Europe. But he knew he did not have time for personal pleasures.

As the helicopter set down on the University helipad the Petersons were on hand to greet him. It was not hard for Wang Po to be warm and gracious as he had come to know and like the Petersons even if they were merely pawns in the game he was playing.

"Freda and Hans, it is so good to see you again and I hope that this has not been inconvenient for you to meet with us?" Wang Po proceeded to introduce those he had brought with him as this was the first time they had met in person.

"Not at all, we are pleased to have you with us and to discuss our plans for investigating the Northern Lights problem. We have asked Jars Svenson to join as well since we will be going to his archaeological site outside of Tromso as this seems to have been the center of some unusual magnetic changes which are part of the investigation."

"Excellent, the more help we can have the better and I only hope we can come up with answers as to why this is happening." Wang Po commented as they climbed into the van to go to the Peterson's lab on the university campus. In the distance he did not see the telescope that was trained on them from the university tower through which Harry Roberts was watching.

Dame Walters had already clued him in that Wang Po was not what he appeared, and she already suspected he had was involved in the loss of the tender on which they knew he was having a meeting. Unfortunately, they were unable to hear what transpired at the meeting because of screening that prevented their penetration of the meeting. That in itself raised a red flag. You did not create electronic interference to prevent someone hearing your conversation about an innocent operation. And Wang Po was known to MI6 and the CIA to be a serious player in the military wing of the CPC. He would not be involved in something that was purely commercial or scientific. And his diplomatic status was merely a cover protecting him should things go wrong in Norway.

Taking pictures of the group Harry was already sending these to London to identify all those meeting with the Petersons. As for the Chinese grant to the Petersons they already knew of this as the Petersons had been careful to disclose the information to their university and government of Norway but were told to keep that knowledge to themselves. They would be in no trouble because of the grants but it was obvious by the way they were arranged this was intended as later to be used for blackmail or to undermine the Petersons, whichever was to the CPC's advantage. Harry and Dame Walters were making sure that would never happen.

Chapter Four

Echo II was refueled and provisioned and ready for its trip north to Tromso. Even in the late summer months all on board were going to have heavy jackets and gear for dealing with both the cold climate in the far north and the very cold waters of the north Atlantic.

Harold and Ming Lee were putting final touches on improvements they were making to the AUV from Kongsberg Marine, and they had spent the day meeting with the company to be sure they had the latest software in place as well as security.

After the fiasco in the Rhone River searching for the Arles Wreck when the drone AUV had been hacked they wanted to be sure that was not possible again. The same was true of the surveillance drones.

They had four of the overhead surveillance drones on board to be able to observe multiple sights. All were the advanced versions capable of unlimited flight time with their solar power and the speed, climb rate and altitude had all been improved. While great before the new drones were even more advanced.

Meg and Harold usually did this work but now that Ming Lee was part of the team, she had taken over some of the duties. An engineer, she and Harold were working well together and while Meg missed being involved day to day, she knew it was important to let them develop a partnership in their work as well as personal lives.

Recently they had discovered a previously unknown back door into the software for the AUV which they now had closed. With technology you could never be sure you were safe from hacking, but they felt they were as close as they would come, at least for now. But it was a continuous process. Sort of like the old children's game of Whack a Mole, when you hammered down one area of risk another seemed to pop up.

"What about that latest update on the software from Kongsberg?" Ming Lee asked Harold.

"Uploaded it last night and seems to be working well. I am glad they substituted the newest AUV for the older one and they have really been great to work with solving all our problems."

"I am sure they appreciate our help in this as well; it really has been a joint effort to make improvements, especially in security."

"What about the stealth capability as well as ability to send out false GPS coordinates?"

"Again, all in place and with considerable improvements since the last time we used this off the Chinese islands in the South China Sea."

The talk turned from technology to their new flat they were renting together in Oxford and to the trip they planned to Scotland to meet his parents. Ming Lee was still uneasy about Harold meeting her traditional Chinese parents in Australia. They had all fled Hong Kong and taken their British citizenship with them. With developments on the mainland and in Hong Kong, Ming Lee was greatly relieved that she had finally talked her parents into emigrating. They were slowly making a new life for themselves just outside of Sydney.

Her father, a professor of engineering, was teaching now at the University of Sydney and had been given tenure and full professorship in the last year. He was even awarded teacher of the year last year. Fact that he spoke excellent English went over well with the students who often had trouble with Chinese and Indian instructors who were not fluent in English.

Her mother, now that Ming Lee there only child, was grown had started an online business selling jewelry and was having amazing success with her start up. For someone who hated computers when living in Hong Kong she had taken to them as a business opportunity as Ming Lee would never have guessed possible. She was even making use of all the social media outlets to expand the business.

Harold's mother had been in contact with Ming Lee's mother and to the surprise of all they seem to have hit it off. Between daily e mails and occasional facetime talks Harold's mother had been helping Ming Lee's mother with the business as she too was doing an online business in Scottish woolens. They were even talking of combining their businesses. Harold and Ming Lee could not have been happier that the two families were getting along. Of course, the fact that Harold's father was also an engineer gave he and Ming Lee's father something in common.

Still, Ming Lee worried about longer term when they found out how serious she and Harold were and their plans for the future. But that was for another day. Today they would be heading north to investigate the strange events surrounding changes in the magnetic field and the Northern Lights. More and more they were convinced that they two events were somehow related, and Ming Lee was almost certain that the Chinese CPC was somehow involved.

When Ming Lee and Harold came topside to the bridge to report on their status to Harry and

Fred, they found them talking with Captain Hastings about potential ice bergs that seemed to be breaking off with increasing frequency from the polar ice cap. While Echo II had been refitted for light ice breaking it was far from an ice breaker though they did not think there would be any need for ice breaking. Dodging large chucks of ice bergs mostly hidden below the surface was something else.

Norway was advanced in its surveillance of these ice bergs but there was always the risk of one stray that they missed. Hopefully Echo II would miss them as well.

From icebergs the talk turned to assigning staterooms to the new passengers. Freda and Hans Peterson would be coming on board shortly and Jars Svenson was already settling into his cabin. Adjustments had to be made as some of the crew would have to bunk together on this trip with so many people on board. Fortunately, Craig Rathbone, Director of the CIA was not on board yet although Dame Walters said he was flying to Tromso today and would be joining them in a few days.

Dame Walters had enlisted his aid on the project after learning that there was more involved here than just a scientific inquiry into the Northern Lights. Craig was concerned about the impact on the satellite system as well as the GPS system that changes in magnetic field might cause. Craig had been on board Echo II numerous times in the past and, along with Dame Walters, was god parent to two of the three children. Craig was a friend, but when it came to security matters he was all business, as was Dame Walters.

As it seemed they had all in order to begin their journey north all but Captain Hastings retired to the James quarters which Fred and Angelique had maintained as their private home on the water. Earl James as they now knew him and Lady Angelique had transformed the quarters into a real home over the years. While their homes in London and Oxford were their frequent residences, they enjoyed being on Echo II most of all. When they came into the dining room Martin Fredricks and Sally were chatting with Angelique over tea.

"Please, come and join us?" Angelique had the attendant bring another pot of tea. She had learned Ming Lee's particular taste in tea, and they shared a love of trying new varieties. Harold on the other hand was not a great fan so she had coffee for him as well.

"Harold how are things coming with the AUV and drones?" Martin asked.

"We are ready and plan to deploy the drones over the archaeological site as soon as we are near to Tromso. Also, one over the Nordic Prince drill rig in deep water that the Chinese are operating. They took this over from Shell Oil earlier this year. No one is allowed on the rig other than Chinese workers and they have a defense set up around the rig. We will deploy the AUV but want to be careful not to run afoul of their defense until we know what is going on."

Ming Lee let Harold hold forth on the technology and Angelique noted how smoothly Ming Lee was helping to build Harold's confidence. He was inherently shy and reserved but Ming Lee was bringing him out of his shell and obviously was good for him. And he for her. Harold was more than supportive of her work and they shared both a work and personal partnership that was a pleasure to see develop.

Angelique had to chuckle to herself that Echo II once more seemed to have brought a couple together. First it was John and Liz Peters and Harry and Meg Roberts searching for Alexander's tomb. Then it was Nicos and Maria in the search for the Devil's Dagger and preventing the spread of a deadly virus. Next were she and Fred James when Echo II was searching for the Arles Wreck in Arles, France where she was Mayor. Now it appeared Ming Lee and Harold had become a couple after their adventure in the South China Sea preventing development of an EMP device that could have changed the balance of power in the world. They might yet have to change Echo II to Love Boat II she thought. And she had notice that Captain Hastings seemed to be spending more and more time with his new First Officer Angela Davis who he had recruited with Martin Fredrick's help when she had left the Navy last year.

Angelique looking around the table was glad they had bought a new dining room table that could be modified from seating twelve to up to twenty.
And Fred's steward, who had been with him for years, was a real treasure who Angelique relied on to arrange dinners and take care of the quarters. She had asked Fred where he had found Philip and he had been the cabin steward for Fred and Martin when they shared a cabin as midshipmen in the Navy and ended up with Fred as he advanced to the rank of Captain before leaving the Navy.

As she was musing over these matters John and Liz came in to join for tea. John, an American, had become fond of British teatime while Liz being British had no adjustment to make. With them was Jars Svenson who was preparing to take them to the archaeological site outside

Tromso and who had brought with him a chart of the site.

Laying the chart out on the table Jars was pointing out all the features of the site, what had been done and the work they were planning to do. It seemed that while the site was now inland at one time it adjoined the sea. They hoped to find remains of Viking ships at the site and had already discovered significant tombs that remained undisturbed from the earliest days of the Vikings. Indications were that this site was one from which the Vikings had launched ships for Iceland and beyond as some items found were native to Iceland so returning ships had brought items back to Norway.

Jars went on to give a bit of Viking history. It was always surprising to find how widespread the Vikings were in their travels. Not only west to Iceland, Greenland and what is now Canada but also deep into Europe including Russia and Turkey. Runes were carved as graffiti in places in the church, and now a mosque, of Hagia Sophia in Istanbul as Vikings had been hired as mercenaries for Emperor Constantine in what is now Turkey.

Of course, most knew of the Viking history in England and France where the Normans were of Viking origin. The site they were now going to explore had only begun to be excavated and Jars was pleased that Harold had brought along their deep penetrating ground radar system as well as the drone having LIDAR capability. The ability to see features without digging would be of immense value and save time and money doing excavations.

"How big was the site do you think when it was active?" Harold asking, thinking ahead to the investigation.

"We estimate it covered some three miles square with population of perhaps some 5000 people which, for that time in the north of Norway, was significant. In fact, it was probably one of the most populated villages. We think they were particularly interested in seals and whales as need for oil was significant before modern times.

"I am surprised to know that whales are this far north!" Ming Lee was interested in whales and had been studying them for years.

"You might find this website of interest Ming Lee. They have expeditions to see the ORCA whales and even scuba diving with them though I am not recommending that." Jars gave her the website to one of the groups doing whale watching trips. https://www.orcanorway.info/

Jars went on to explain that from October through January outside of Tromso, Norway is found the largest collection of killer whales in the world.   The reason apparently is the feast of herring available to them.   Not only do Norwegians like their pickled herring but the ORCA seem to like them as much or more.   It always surprises people that the Tromso region in the very north of Norway is the best place to do whale watching.

"We are out of season right now, but we may still see some on the trip. But you will have to come back and do a whale trip one day." Harold and Ming Lee smiled thinking that this November might be perfect time for a trip to see the whales.

Chapter Five

Being early fall the weather was brisk as the Echo II made its way north to the top of Norway and Tromso. Instead of spending time on deck most passengers and crew stayed inside watching the coast go by from the lounge viewing windows.

Fred and Martin spent part of the trip discussing the convoys that operated in this area during WWII on their way to Murmansk in Russia, which was the same latitude and just around the top of Norway. Not far in fact in miles from Tromso although over the mountain range. German fighters and U boats decimated the early convoys with one in ten freighters lucky to make a safe trip.

Jars and John and Liz spent much of their time going over the chart of the archaeological site while Ming Lee and Meg spent time discussing with Jars the anomaly that was occurring in the magnetic field at the site.

"One of the concerns with changes in the magnetic field is the fact that the US armed forces as well as their allies have been in the process of substituting positioning by use of the magnetic field for GPS. The concern is the loss of GPS satellites in the event of a major war. According to Defense One, "Accurate and extremely difficult to jam, the magnetic field could be used as a means of navigation for ground troops, ships at sea, and aircraft. The magnetic field could also guide missiles to their targets with an accuracy of just over 30 feet."

Even today it is a problem. In 2019 pilots found the Russians were jamming GPS in the middle east affecting flights from Cyprus to Israel and various countries have been developing jamming, spoofing and other ways of interfering with the GPS satellite system.

Meg went on to explain more. "While using the magnetic field is a bit less accurate it is far less able to be tampered with. Unless of course the Chinese have found a way to do that and that is one of the reasons that MI6 and the CIA are concerned and involved in investigating what is happening here in Norway."

"Is there any way to interfere with the use of the magnetic field for navigation and positioning?" Harry asked.

"It would probably be less useful in case of a nuclear war. A nuclear explosion could jam the MAGNAV system as the use of the magnetic field for navigation is called. But for conventional conflicts there is no known way at the moment for jamming this system of positioning.

Harold added his thoughts. "Another problem is how you get magnetic maps of your enemy territory. One possibility is to use your magnetic maps up to a border and then switch to the less reliable inertial navigation system. The Navy has been teaching use of the sextant again just in case that was necessary as a means of navigating without GPS or magnetic mapping."

"But for real accuracy for things like cruise missiles, GPS or magnetic mapping is invaluable. So, if there has been found a way to jam or spoof the magnetic mapping system we need to know."

Harold went on to explain that the military has been concerned over GPS for some time and working on all kinds of alternatives including quantum clocks. In 2017 an assistant professor at the Air Force Academy published a paper about making use of the magnetic field for positioning. https://ieeexplore.ieee.org/document/7808987 and while a plane's own electrical signals could interfere with accurate positioning use of artificial intelligence has made possible cancelling out noise and making more accurate readings.

More work has been done at MIT. https://arxiv.org/abs/2007.12158 and of course one worry is the presence of Chinese students in engineering at MIT as well as grants to professors sourced from China. Not only might this give them the technology but might also give them a way to negate the use of the technology for military purposes.

Meg pointed out that continuing developments in artificial intelligence would likely reduce the risk of jamming and increase the accuracy of a MAGNAV system. And if an enemy knew that you had this back up in place jamming the GPS system would be less advantageous to them. At the moment the MAGNAV system is only slightly less accurate than GPS.

"It has been known for years that animals often use their own form of MAGNAV for orientation and navigation. Sea turtles and birds are just two animals making use of magnetoreception so we are just catching up with what many in the animal kingdom have been doing for eons." Meg added bringing up and showing an example of a map of the earth's magnetic field.

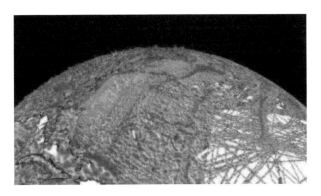

NOAA map of the magnetic anomaly field

"While MAGNAV has a long way to go before it is universally implemented, if it every is, there is considerable study of its potential." Meg pulled up several websites discussing the subject so that all on board had a chance to familiarize themselves with the science to better be prepared to deal with whatever they might find at Tromso.

"Jars why don't tell us just what you have been observing at the Tromso site you have been working."

"Sure, the GPS has been fine. We have used that to map the site and mark locations with geomarkers. But when we try to use a compass the needle swings wildly at times. At other times it works just fine. There seems to be no reason for why this is happening. We have tried to correlate it with solar flares, but nothing seems to line up to give us an explanation. And this started happening while the Northern Lights began to intensify and appear more regularly."

Jars went on, "that is the reason I contacted the Petersons to see if they had any idea what was going on. So far, we have no explanation. It also started just about the time that the Chinese took over the Nordic Prince oil drilling rig just off the coast. Because that is in international waters and outside of the Norwegian economic zone, we have not been able to investigate on the rig itself."

He went on, "the Chinese have come up with all kinds of reasons not to allow us on the rig. They claim there are safety issues and once resolved we will be welcome. But it seems there is one issue after another denying us entry."

While it was possible this was all an innocent correlation the more coincidences that were piling up Harold said that he was suspicious the Chinese were once more involved in something of concern. But finding out what was going to be difficult and proving it even harder.

The discussion continued for some time with Meg pulling up various webpages for review and Jars explaining more about the readings they had been getting on the magnetic field. It was suggested that they have a new reading of the general area including the Nordic Prince to see if the magnetic anomaly maps before and now showed a difference. Dame Walters made calls to get that started.

Meg, Harold and Ming Lee went to the technology bay of the ship and began to program the drones sending one to the archaeology site and another to the Nordic Prince. Both were programmed to reach their destination and then to continuously monitor activity. They had added a capability for the drones to monitor any changes in the magnetic field from what was to be expected although they were not entirely sure that this would work as it was a new design and untested before. At least the infra

red would give them an idea if there were any unexpected visitors to the archaeological site known as Viking 18 and how many personnel were on the Nordic Prince.

They decided to hold off on launching the AUV to inspect the Nordic Prince. While it was likely that the Chinese were aware of Echo II and its activities, they wanted for now to keep a bit lower profile. The drones overhead will give them what they need for the moment.

Arriving at Tromso in the early evening they decided to have dinner on board and discuss plans for the next day. Jars along with the Petersons, John and Liz were off to the Viking 18 site taking Ming Lee and Harold along to get readings on the magnetic field and see if any new anomalies were showing up. They would also review the readings that were being taken regularly on the site.

Harry and Meg would spend the day along with Fred and Angelique and Martin and Susan, Nicos and Maria touring the city. They were surprised how large a city it was this far north in Norway. They wanted to get a good feel for the city and acting like tourists seemed advisable.

Dame Walters begged off the tour of the city saying she had a meeting with Craig Rathbone scheduled as he had sent a text that he had arrived in Tromso and would be joining them on the Echo II later in the day.

Little did anyone know then what this day would bring.

Chapter Six

Jars arranged for the Viking 18 bus to pick everyone up at the Echo II for the short trip to the site of the dig. Ming Lee and Harold loaded up their equipment and brought with them the remote equipment from the drone that was continuously monitoring the site. While they had seen spikes in the magnetic readings earlier, at the moment those seemed to have died down with only normal readings since Echo II left Oslo.

Jars spent the trip more as tour guide explaining the work they were doing and the chance to uncover yet another nearly intact Viking warship that ground penetrating radar had found. He was hoping the new equipment Ming Lee and Harold were bringing would give them an even better view of the ship as well as the village which dated from the time of Eric the Red.

Ming Lee asked Jars about Erick the Red as she knew little of Viking history. He explained that he lived from 950 to 1003 CE it is believed. His actual name was Erik Thyorvaldsson and was the founder of the first European settlement in Greenland around c.985. He is also the father of Lief Erikson believed to have been one of the first Europeans to reach North America.

"We are hoping with your help to verify the age of the settlement and perhaps turn up more revealing information on Erik the Red."   Jars continued. John and Liz knew the background but Ming Lee and Harold both peppered Jars with questions about the Vikings and the era of the settlement.

It took only about an hour and a half to reach the site of the work and the first thing John and Liz noted was how little work had been done. Beyond staking out boundaries and setting up a small work shed as well as an open-air covered work area no actual excavation seemed to be underway.

"Jars, I thought you are making more progress than what I am seeing. "   John commented.

"Yes, we have been hampered by weather and also difficulty in finding workers to help. The new financing you helped us get should allow us to speed this up before winter sets in. That is our hope."

"I hope so too. I am anxious to see the site where you think the ship is located." Liz added as she watched Ming Lee and Harold setting up the new ground penetrating radar and moving it to the site where the ship was indicated by the earlier work.

It did not take long for Ming Lee and Harold to get started and Ming Lee was running the radar over the site "mowing the lawn" as it was called, going back and forth in carefully planned tracks to give a clear picture of what lay below. Harold was on the computer watching and building the tracks into a composite.   Liz was looking over his shoulder and was pleased to see the detail of the ship was coming up with amazing clarity.

"We hope to excavate the ship first but before then we need to build the container that will prevent the wood from deteriorating once it is unearthed. That is, as you know Liz, the tricky part when dealing with long buried items of wood. We will submerge it in water mixed with chemicals that will begin to stabilize the wood. The container is due to be delivered here in the next few days."

"I assume you will not do any excavating until you have that set up." John commented.

"Yes, and that is part of what has slowed us down."

"Jars I need you to show us the readings you are getting on the magnetic field and I want Ming

Lee and Harold once done with the ship to start checking the current readings." This from Hans Peterson who with his wife Freda were walking to the shed that had been set up as a temporary work area for the dig.

While Jars had brought some readings with him to show everyone on Echo II there were far more in the work shed to be reviewed. Hans pulled a compass from his pocket and checked but saw nothing strange as the needle pointed clearly north as expected. Jars had told him that on occasion compass readings here had violently swung one direction and another. But that was not the case now.

On the trip to Viking 18 when Jars was not giving history lesson on the Vikings and the site of Viking 18 the Petersons were outlining the problems with the magnetic field.

"The field is believed to be created by the internal movement of molten iron in the earth's core resulting from the rotation of the earth. Fingerprints in the rock structure tell the story that every 200,000 to 300,000 years the poles reverse. This does not happen overnight, but over thousands of years."

Hans went on to explain. "While it has not happened now for nearly 800,000 years there are signs it could be happening now. For one thing the magnetic field is wobbling more than usual. Another is the movement of the Northern Lights to areas more southerly than would usually see them. The same true of the Southern Lights moving north. And while this is helpful for tourism it is also a sign that the magnetic field is protecting the earth less from solar radiation raising risk of increasing cancers and effects on agriculture."

Freda added that, "while eventually the south pole will become north when compasses are used and vice versa it is the weakening of the field that is perhaps the greatest concern. Some have posited that climate change has something to do with the changes, but it is more likely a cyclical development as it has been going on for millions of years. Long before man became a factor. That said it is important to determine if there is any possibility that the change in magnetic field is simply a force of nature or if there is perhaps something else involved."

While Ming Lee and Harold were mowing the lawn with their ground penetrating radar Lars was taking everyone else on a tour of the site pointing out what they had discovered so far and what they were hoping to find.

"We hope to locate even more burial grounds as it is likely there we will find artifacts worthy of display at the museum as well as having historical value. In addition, we hope to trace the trade patterns of these early Vikings. What led them to make the sea voyage to Iceland, Greenland and eventually to North America. We know so little of what caused them to venture from their homeland."

John and Liz discussed what help Jars needed to complete the survey and excavation and what timetable he was on. They discussed sources of funding as well as the work John and Liz could do with their students from Oxford.

Meanwhile the Petersons, after having gone through most of the site, went back to the excavation shed to study the logs of the changes noted in the magnetic fields taking numerous photos of the logs to be studied when they returned to the university.

Freda commented to Hans, "Did you note the pattern in the log?" Hans nodded and added "Yes there seems to be a consistency to when the anomalies occurred. Seems like for two days once a month, although the particular days seem to vary. But no more than two days at a time.

"That seem inconsistent with a natural pattern don't you think?" The question from Freda was rhetorical.

On the Nordic Prince drilling platform Wang Po had been listening to the Petersons from a bug that had been planted in the expedition work shed some time ago to monitor activities. Likewise, he had been hearing much of the conversations of Jars from a satellite dish installed in the tree line adjoining the site.

His jaw tightened as he realized that the Peterson's were not going to be misled by the varied pattern of the changes in the field as he had hoped. The objective here was to make they concluded that this was simply a function of a natural change that had been occurring over the life of the planet.

"Damn! Why could they not accept the conclusions of that journal article we had planted and let this go." He realized he had spoken aloud but then there was no one in the control room to hear him. Still, it annoyed him.

Wang Po picked up the phone and talked to the new supervisor of the rig making sure that he did nothing until told to begin work again. He did not want any new observations while the Petersons were in the area. And he decided he needed to be more proactive with Echo II in Tromso. But it needed to appear unrelated to the Nordic Prince or his involvement in the area.

He had several options. Picking up the phone again he gave orders wondering if this was really the time to do more than monitor and whether he should involve Beijing in the decision. But he knew that Beijing would only tell him it was his responsibility and seeking advice he would appear weak. Something he could never afford.

By noon Jars had shown John and Liz all they needed to see of the site. Ming Lee and Harold had completed their survey which they were going over with Jars who seemed extremely pleased with the results. The ship appeared to be even larger than the one on display in the museum and appeared to be in excellent condition.

Jars immediately put in a call to have the container brought to the site that would be used to protect the ship once it was unearthed. He also called his PR department sending them a copy of the results and suggesting a press release. The museum always needed funding and there was nothing more helpful in loosening the wallets than press reports of a new and exciting discovery.

John and Liz shared a smile as they understood the politics of museums and research. Sadly, they lived or died based on the excitement they could generate from donors. It was a fact of live in their world. One you came to realize early in your career and, if you were smart, you learned to play the game. Besides there was excitement in a new discovery for those making the discovery as well as their benefactors.

Jars suggested that they head back to the city for lunch and as it had started to rain he felt they probably had done all they could do today. Ming Lee and Harold loaded their equipment and the Petersons finished up photographing the log.

It was a couple of miles on the road back to Tromso when the bus came to a screeching halt as the driver turned a corner to find a tree had fallen over the road. He and Jars got out of the bus to examine and Jars was on the phone when gun fire erupted. Jars was struck in the chest and it was obvious he was killed instantly. The driver ran into the woods with shots following him until he too was brought down.

Inside the bus John as on the phone to Fred and Harry calling for help. He considered opening the back door of the bus and having everyone scatter but considering what happened to Jars and the driver that seemed a foolish idea. They were trapped.

The gunmen entered the bus with black hoods and spoke in Norwegian which fortunately the Petersons understood. The others knew only a few words. It was obvious from the discussion that this was a robbery. Wallets, rings, watches and phones were all demanded and put in sacks that were handed around. The gunmen then took the Petersons off the bus and into the woods. It was only a few minutes before shots rang out and John decided that he had to act.

Quickly getting the bus in gear he reversed and spun the bus around at the first opportunity heading back to the Viking 18 site. He hoped that Harry or Fred had gotten the authorities involved and that help was on the way. Ming Lee and Harold were on their computers watching the drone activity and moving the drone from the site to overhead to see if the gunmen were following them.   The only good news was there was no pursuit.

It made no sense. Why would a robbery turn violent killing two and probably four people? John had the strong feeling this had less to do with a robbery than with the reason they were in Norway. While made to appear to be common banditry the killings made that unlikely. Especially the Petersons who were the lead scientists studying the Northern Light – magnetic field anomalies. It was just too convenient. Yet, what did they know that could call for such drastic action?

John quickly gathered up all the magnetic field logs and had Ming Lee and Harold enter pix into their computers and upload them. The Petersons had taken pictures on their phones but those were gone now. Surely there was nothing in the logs that significant or they would have mentioned something. But perhaps there was more here than they knew so best to preserve these logs. If they were important then someone would obviously come to either take or destroy them so having copies now was important.

"Any signs of pursuit from the drones?" John asked Harold.

"No, so far nothing. We did turn on the infrared and could trace the killers as they left the woods but having gotten in a vehicle they are long gone now. Unfortunately, we did see four bodies with no movement and while warm enough to show up on the infrared they are cooling so I think we can assume they are all dead or dying." Harold was clearly shaken. Ming Lee having been part of MI6 was staying collected but this was Harold's first experience with violence firsthand. Not that you ever got used to senseless violence, John thought.

Overhead they heard the sound of a helicopter and hoped that this was coming to their rescue. Not long until they could see the red cross on the side and once landing John had quickly had them leave for the site of the shootings in case Jars or the Petersons or the driver were still alive. Two armed SAS employees Harry had sent from the Echo II stayed on site and two others went with the helicopter.   The radio from the other site was turned up by the SAS operative standing next to John and it was clear that there was nothing that could be done for Jars or the others. From what had started out a happy day for Jars had turned into disaster.

What was worrying John the most was the real reason was behind the attack. He was not buying robbery as a motive and he knew this was only the start of trouble if whoever was behind this was willing to engage in this level of violence at this point in the investigation.

Chapter Seven

Back on Echo II Meg was reviewing the drone footage that was stationary over the Chinese oil rig Nordic Prince. She was looking at the infrared readings and her anger grew as she noted that three people left the rig prior to the bus attack and in time to have been the perpetrators. Likewise, three people returned to the rig in a time that fit with their having made the attack and return. Of course, there was no way this would help law enforcement to apprehend those responsible. But it did confirm what they all assumed and that was this was no simple robbery and murder. But just what the Chinese were hiding that would call for such drastic action was still unclear.

"Fred, I think we need to move Echo II closer to the Nordic Prince and use the AUV to see just what defenses they have set up and also see if we can figure out just what they are up to." Meg commented as she passed on the information to John and Liz who were still shaken from the afternoon events and getting increasingly angry. Meg knew that best thing she could do now was give them something focus on. Same with Harold. Ming Lee on the other hand having been involved in skirmishes before was composed although she too was angry.

"John, I have made arrangements for Jars and Petersons to be taken back to Oslo when the bodies are released. Jars was single and no children but sadly the Petersons had two children. I have found they do have grandparents to take care of them and have set up a trust fund for them." Fred who was a British Earl and immensely wealthy would make sure the children were cared for. He was a compassionate man as was his wife Angelique. This was just one more example of their caring for people. Their charitable works were well known, if done mostly anonymously.

"Thanks Fred, I know that will help but losing your parents at young age is hard on any child. I cannot believe how angry I am at the Chinese right now. Frankly, it is good we do not have weapons on that drone, or I might be tempted to take out that Nordic Prince." Fred had never seen Harold this angry or upset but it was understandable. Ming Lee was wisely just letting him come to terms with what happened.

It took a couple of hours to get Echo II underway but would not take them more than a few hours to get in close enough to the Nordic Prince and launch the AUV. The days of ROV which were tethered to an oceanographic ship were ending with the autonomous underwater vehicles (AUV) that could go for days doing their work surfacing occasionally to transmit data. Not only was it cheaper to operate but software that analyzed the data made it so much easier than having someone sit watching hour after hour of mud on sea bottoms as happened with the tethered ROV in the earlier days.

Harold and Meg were in the equipment bay with Ming Lee going over the new Kongsberg AUV they planned to launch.

"I think we should just operate this remotely and not try to program it. Best we stand off and circle the platform before moving in closer. You can be sure they have defense and monitors set up and while the stealth technology is improved there is no assurance they will not spot us. Last thing we want is to lose this AUV. I think even Fred would gulp if he had to buy this as it is millions of dollars in equipment." But they knew that Fred was aware of the risk and probably would send the bill to MI6 anyway.

Meg was thinking out loud as she made final adjustments and check on the AUV. Ming Lee was handling the computer check while Harold was adjusting the various settings.

The Hugin AUV was a technological marvel and such an advance over early AUV or ROV methods of doing underwater research. And they were so lucky to be here in Norway where they company was based. Meg, Harold and Ming Lee were all looking forward to spending time with the headquarters group to discuss the AUV and to meet in person those who had been so helpful in supplying and adjusting the AUV for them. So far, they had only been talking by phone or e mail or text. It would be good to meet Alf Anderson who had been their contact with the company.

Ming Lee was looking at the company website describing the benefits of the AUV. https://www.kongsberg.com/maritime/products/marine-robotics/autonomous-underwater-vehicles/AUV-hugin/

Key features

- Very stable and low noise hydrodynamic platform for payload sensors
- High maneuverability providing terrain following and turning radius of 15 metres
- Operating depths of 3000, 4500 and 6000 metres
- Operator supervised ("acoustic tether"), semiautonomous or autonomous operation
- State of the art Aided Inertial Navigation System (AINS)
- Provides robustness and sound technical solutions to the demands of modern navies

- Latest battery technology with up to 100 hours endurance at 4 knots
- Highly flexible configuration and integration of payload systems
- Typical payload sensors are synthetic aperture sonar or side-scan sonar, multibeam echo sounder, sub-bottom profiler, camera, CTD and volume search sonar

For their use they had worked with Alf to modify the AUV especially to provide a stealth capability. But also, to limit the ability to hack and to be able to send out false GPS and other signals. This had been so helpful with working in the Rhone River several years ago.

Back in the lounge Harry was going over with John and Liz what happened on the bus. He was kicking himself for not sending some of his SAS team with them. But he knew that no one thought there was a danger on that trip to the archaeological site. He also knew that he had made a mistake, when dealing with the Chinese you had to always anticipate trouble. He would not make this mistake again.

"We will make them pay for this, be sure of that. But it will not bring Jars or the Petersons back." Harry was convinced from what Meg had showed him that the Chinese were behind the attack. He was glad that Ming Lee, Harold and the Peters were all safe. He knew that MI6 would not give him the latitude it wanted to take out the Nordic Prince, but he was tempted anyway. Still, he knew they had to find out what they were up to before taking any drastic action. He was a professional and could not let his anger cloud his judgment. Not now.

"Did you share what we know with the local authorities?" Liz asked.

"No, I talked to Dame Walters and she did not think that was wise at this point. She was giving the background to her counterpart in the Norwegian secret service who asked to be kept in the loop. I would not be surprised if they do not join us at some point."

The steward walked by with boxes in which he had put the effects of Jars and the Petersons that had been in their staterooms and all were quiet as they realized what he was doing.

It was early evening when Echo II was in position and launched the AUV. All were watching the monitors as it circled the Nordic Prince. They were about a quarter mile from the rig and could see its underwater lights. Harold and Ming Lee were noting that they were being pinged with sonar but were convinced that their stealth technology was working and that they were not being detected. But it was clear as they suspected that this was no ordinary drilling platform.

"There is enough light for us to see the drill apparatus under the platform and that is one unusual set up. I have never seen a drilling operation with the pipe that diameter. It must be a good twenty-four inches in diameter. Pretty clear they are not looking for oil." Meg was taking photographs as they circled the rig getting closer and closer to the platform.

"I think that is about all we are going to see tonight. Let's get the AUV back on board." Meg was talking with Harold.

"Time to head back to Oslo and meet with Dame Walters and Craig Rathbone and see what they have learned and what we need to do next." Harry was commenting to Fred who gave the word to his Captain to head for Oslo once the AUV was back on board.

Chapter Eight

On board the Nordic Prince Wang Po was berating the team he sent to Tromso to deal with the problem.

"I never told you to kill anyone! The idea was only to put a scare into them. Now they will suspect something is going on. Damned fools, you will be returned to China immediately for disciplinary action and you can expect your families to suffer the same fate as awaits you. Get out of my sight!"

The three men departed as quickly as they could but being under guard knew their fate was sealed. They thought they understood what Wang Po wanted; obviously not. They dreaded their fate when returned to China. As well they should.

Wang Po debated his next steps. He knew he should notify Beijing, but he knew he would be in as much or more trouble than the three men. He picked up the phone and talked to the head of his security detail. Better that the three men be eliminated here tonight than to return them to China, despite what he had told them. Fortunately, the incinerator on the Nordic Prince would eliminate all trace of the men who would just be reported missing. The Nordic Prince could be a dangerous place to work.

The next morning Echo II was docked once more in Oslo. John and Liz debated calling on the grandparents of the Peterson children but decided it was not the right time. Besides, it was probably more important to avenge their deaths than to try and console the grandparents or children. Better they spend their time finding out what had happened and why.

At breakfast Dame Walters and Craig Rathbone joined everyone to discuss what had happened in Tromso and the next steps.

"I guess we should have anticipated the Chinese reaction, but I never thought there would danger to anyone this early. The fact they reacted as they have needs to put us on high alert." Dame Walters expressed what everyone had thought.

Fred had already increased security on Echo II and their defenses were increased to the highest level. Echo II was not a warship, but it had unusual protection for an oceanographic vessel in view of its past involvement in dangerous work for MI6 and the CIA. A good thing under the circumstances.

"We have already transmitted the data that Meg took off what the Petersons photographed at the site and the preliminary analysis is that what is happening is not a natural phenomenon. We must assume that for whatever reason the Chinese are

once more trying to alter natural forces to gain some advantage for China or a disadvantage for those they perceive as enemies." Craig and Dame Walters had obviously been busy.

"With the loss of the Petersons, who were leading experts on the magnetic field and its interrelationship with the Northern Lights, we have been reaching out for more information. I think it is important for us to understand what we are dealing with." Craig paused to take a sip of coffee but more important to be sure everyone was paying attention before he continued.

"Ok, the earth is essentially a magnet with a south and north pole. The field begins at the south pole for the moment and extends around the earth interacting to some extent with other galactic fields and then reenters the earth at the north pole. As to how this is generated, we must understand that at the center of the earth is a solid core outside of which is a hot liquid layer. The earth is trying since its formation to shed itself of this heat and doing so by convection. And convection generates electric current in the molten layer and that in turn creates a magnetic field." Craig paused again to make sure everyone was with him.

"This field is being created and destroyed regularly and reaches out thousands of miles into space. It is our planet's defense against solar radiation that would otherwise make life here impossible. Mars on the other hand lost its shield eons ago and therefore is exposed to that radiation in a way that does not happen on earth."

"So far so good. From study of rocks in the earth's crust we know that the poles have reversed many times in the history of the earth with some regularity but without our knowing just when it might occur. Of course, the magnetic field to us is invisible unlike various birds and other creatures who have a way of interacting with the magnetic field. Other than our compasses the only time we detect the field is when we see an aurora or the Northern or Southern Lights. These are oxygen and nitrogen molecules that when they are excited and then relax are giving off light. That excitement comes from radiation particles from the sun interacting with our atmosphere. These occur close to the poles because of the strength of the poles. At least that is what the scientists tell me. I must admit to not understanding a lot of what I was being told."

Craig went on to explain that, "those concerned about a polar flip worry that it will weaken the magnetic field at least temporarily allowing more solar radiation to strike the earth causing cancers and other issues such as changes to climate and agriculture. But typically, the change would not occur overnight but over an exceptionally long period of time. Thousands of years. At least that is what they think, though of course no one in recorded history has had this happen so it is purely speculation on their part. But this is why the concern over the changes in the Northern Lights indicating there has been some change in the field."

"So, the auroras are basically magnetism made visible?" Harold asked and Craig nodded.

"But then why do we only see these in the very north or the very south and only occasionally further south?" Meg was curious to know.

"It turns out that the sun has its own magnetic field and when its field interacts with earth it squeezes our magnetic field and does so in non-uniform ways. As a result, the auroras in the north and south differ most of the time and only rarely look similar. As for why auroras extend further south at times (or north in the Southern Hemisphere) it is when there are larger bursts of solar energy. The plasma from the sun travels north and south along our magnetic lines and disrupts the oxygen atoms the most the further toward the poles." Craig thought he had it right, but he still did not understand clearly what the scientists had explained to him about the effect of the sun on the magnetic field.

"Let me see if I understand." Harold said. "The concern we have is that we are seeing the aurora much further south right now and there is no solar activity that would account for it?"

"Exactly, to see the aurora as far south as we are seeing it now would normally only result from a massive solar event and there is no such event occurring. This is why there is concern that this may be either something we do not understand or that there may be something that is being done that is affecting the field either intentionally or unintentionally and the chief suspect is the Chinese." Craig explained and waited to see what other questions there might be.

Ming Lee was smiling. She added a comment that was surprising. "You do realize that the Chinese had a compass in use in navigation centuries before the West."

Nicos, not to be outdone and coming from the Greek island of Crete , said that the name "magnet" comes from the Greeks. That some of the purest form of magnetite, the only naturally occurring magnetic material, is found in Thessaly in central Greece. It is said a man name Magnus had his iron shoes and his walking stick held tight by the natural form of magnet that is magnetite, making the discovery of its unique properties.

"Since we are into the arcane of the earth's field did you know that the north pole should actually be the south pole? In a magnet the field runs from north to south but in the case of the earth now it runs the other way around." Harold added at which Ming Lee smiled. She did not say but knew that the Chinese in the beginning used a compass whose orientation was to the south, not the north as in Western compasses. She thought best to keep this to herself.

Craig and Dame Walters seemed amused by the dueling friends and they were pleased to see that they had absorbed the issue and were engaging. It seemed that this problem would take some out of the box thinking and this group of friends were particularly good at that kind of analysis and thinking. But it was time to bring the subject back to the present situation and what to do next.

Dame Walters had a stack of books in front of her and began handing them out.

"This book is an excellent introduction to explain the earth's magnetic field and what we know about polar reversals and changes in the field. I think it would be good bedtime reading for all of us to get us a bit more education."

The book she handed out was by Alanna Mitchell, a science journalist of some repute, and the title was "The Spinning Magnet: The Electromagnetic Force That Created The Modern World –and Could Destroy It."

"The title is a bit over the top with its hint of Armageddon but reading it I think you will find there is quite a bit of good science background. As for possible negative effects if this occurs naturally then there are potential negatives, but they would likely occur over a very long time. On the other hand, if there is some current intentional or unintentional action either environmental or otherwise that could cause harm and it can be stopped that is what we need to know. So, understanding some of the science I think is essential even for those of us who are not scientists. So, start reading!"

Dame Walters smiled but all knew that she was also deadly serious.

The rest of the evening saw everyone quietly reading the book and trying to absorb the science behind both the earth's magnetic field and the aurora phenomenon. The more they read the more puzzled they were about what someone hoped to accomplish if there was an effort being made by the Chinese or others to manipulate the earth's magnetic field. Not only seemingly impossible but if it were possible then the unknown dangers seemed to outweigh any possible advantage that might be gained.

In Australia Dr. Lee was teaching his class when he was called to the office. Once there he was met with the counsel for the CPC who informed him that he was under detention and was to be returned to mainland China. The Provost office was calling the university legal counsel but before they could be reached Dr. Lee was hustled out of the office and into a waiting van.

"I don't understand, I am a British citizen you cannot just take me to mainland China!" Dr. Lee protested to the two men either side of him in the van.

"And yet that is exactly what is going to happen. You will also not like the welcoming committee that has been arranged for you either." The man on his right said with a smug smile just as he injected Dr. Lee with a sedative that would put him to sleep for the duration of the trip.

The CPC plane at a remote airfield was waiting and Dr. Lee was carried to the plane which took off immediately.

The Provost at the university informed both the police and Dr. Lee's wife who immediate sent a text to Ming Lee.

Harold saw Ming Lee tense as she read the message from her mother. She was in shock from what she was reading. She knew that the Chinese took a position that a Chinese national remained Chinese no matter their location or no matter their change of citizenship and remained subject to the law of mainland China. It was like what the Nazis position was with respect to those who had emigrated from the Fatherland. But to risk the ire of Australia over a kidnapping on Australian soil was risky even for the CPC.

She knew that after the Covid crisis that relations between China and Australia were strained at best. Despite China wanting access to Australian minerals and China being a major importer from Australia the Australians had openly defied China demanding an independent investigation of the Wuhan laboratory. Something that China would never agree to.

A second message chilled her even more. It was anonymous but read: "Do not tell your friends about your father. If you do, he will be interred in China for the rest of his life. You will make sure that the investigation you are involved with comes to nothing. If so, your father will be returned unharmed. If not, you will not see your father again. Respond with 'yes' if you understand."

Having no option for the moment she typed yes as instructed. Despite the instructions she allowed Harold to see the messages over her shoulder. Excusing herself she immediately called her mother to assure her that she would do all she could to see her father returned.

Harold was in a quandary. Did he say something to Craig and Dame Walters or the others or remain silent? He waited until Ming Lee returned when he suggested a walk on the deck.

"Ming, I think we need to get Dame Walters involved if for no other reason that protect your mother. They might also try to take her as well." He went on, "and much as you love your father, I know you too well that you would never let this blackmail succeed."

"I know and I have no intention of following their instructions but at the same time I worry that they may have ways of knowing if we tell anyone. I do not know how but these are very technically sophisticated people."

Harold nodded. They had been whispering to each other as couples do just in case they could be overheard. Facing the ocean side they doubted it was possible to hear them remotely on that side of the ship.

"Let me take Harry down to the tech lab where we have that super secure facility. I will write out what is happening and then see his thoughts. I know he will help." Harold was struggling to see how he could help and more than anything he wanted Ming Lee to know she could rely on him. Ming Lee nodded, and Harold went in search of Harry.

Harry understood immediately and was upset that once more he had underestimated the Chinese and how ruthless they could be. After they broke their treaty with Britain on Hong Kong and imprisoned their Muslim population as well as their treatment of Tibet he should not have been surprised. Yet he was.

If they needed any confirmation that this investigation was important, they had just gotten that confirmation. This was a bold and reckless move on the part of the CPC. Harry wrote a quick note back to Harold and went to find Dame Walters and Craig.

Even hardened operatives like Craig and Dame Walters were shocked at the brazenness of the CPS in kidnapping Dr. Lee on Australian soil. It was tantamount to an act of war. Not that

Australia would go to war with China over Dr. Lee. But the government, already stinging from Covid, had to be furious over this assault on their sovereignty.

Both agreed that the less said in messages about this the better. They doubted that the CPC really expected Ming Lee to obey their instructions and that the message was a warning to back off the investigation. Still, they wanted to be careful.

That evening at dinner Craig took special steps to be sure they could not be overheard including having Fred be sure they were in open waters with no ships anywhere around them. A sweep of the ship for listening devices was done regularly during the day in any case.

At the dinner Craig told everyone what was happening. Ming Lee was assured that everything that could be done would be done. But she and they knew that the chances of rescuing her father were slim. Security had been added for her mother though it was bit like closing the barn door after the horse had gotten out. Still as brazen as they had been, they might still try again. Two hostages would be better than one.

It was Ming Lee who spoke next. She had steel in her voice as she assured everyone she had no intention of following the CPC orders and in fact it only made her more resolved to find out what is happening. She suggested that their next move had to be a close surveillance of the Nordic Prince which was only seventy-five miles away from their present location. Fred James agreed and gave instructions to bring the ship within twenty-five miles of the platform.

Chapter Nine

Unknown to any on the Echo II Dr. Lee had not been taken to China. Instead, he was brought to the Nordic Prince. Any attempt to take out the platform would result in his death and at some point Ming Lee would be made aware of that fact. But for the moment his presence on the Nordic Prince would be kept from her. Wang Po knew that his abduction and bringing him on board increased the risk but after the fiasco with the bus he felt he needed the added element until they could complete their work. Also, he hoped to put Dr. Lee's expertise in engineering to work on Project Polar.

Speaking to the platform supervisor Wang Po asked how much longer until the tests were complete, and they could take the final steps. One to two weeks was the response. Provided that Wang Po gave them the go ahead to proceed.

"I suspect that Echo II will surveil us for a while longer, so I want all activity on the special project stopped and make it appear we are doing normal oil drilling. Once they leave the area we will recommence our real work here." With that Wang Po dismissed the man.

That night at dinner Wang Po had Dr. Lee brought to him. "Sit doctor, welcome to the

Nordic Prince. I am sorry for how you were brought here but it was necessary and perhaps you can even be of assistance." Dr. Lee was not fooled by Wang Po who he knew to be one the most ruthless of the scientists working for the CPC. He had no moral compass and, while a man to be feared, he was also no fool.

"By the way, your wife and daughter are both well and aware that we are enjoying your company although they both think you are in mainland China. That can be avoided provided you cooperate with us." The threat was obvious and Dr. Lee nodded while sipping his tea and cautiously eating the dinner provided.

"Just what is it that you wish from me?" Dr. Lee hated fencing with Wang Po but also was curious what he was up to.

"Your background in engineering can be useful to us in the experiments we are carrying out and while I am sure you distrust us; I will tell you that what we are doing here will benefit the entire planet if we are successful. And I am prepared to give you some of the credit provided you cooperate and are helpful in bringing our project to a successful conclusion." Wang Po had decided that involving Dr. Lee could actually be helpful. That was not why he was taken of course but so long as he was here he would be put to work.

Afterward he along with many others would be disposed of. That was the credit he could expect.

"Just what is this project you want my help on?" Dr. Lee had no illusions that he would survive the completion of the project, but he would play along in hopes that he could perhaps derail the project if he found it to be dangerous as he suspected it would be. After all you did not engage in a secret project, kidnap people and kill others as his daughter had informed him happened near Tromso during their bus trip, unless you had something to hide.

"You will see in the morning. For now, enjoy your dinner and get a good night's sleep. Tomorrow we will begin work in preparation to recommence our activities in a few days. This will give you time to learn what you need to know and to help us with our plans." Wang Po was not deceived that Dr. Lee would willingly cooperate but perhaps his curiosity would get him to participate and perhaps even help. We would see. If not, his disposal would be easy to arrange once he had served his purpose as a hostage.

Meanwhile back on Echo II Meg, Liz, Maria and Angelique were all huddled with Ming Lee assuring her that she had all their support, and they would do all they could to make sure her mother and father were safe. Ming Lee knew they meant well but she also knew they had not had the contact with the CPC in China that she had as an MI6 operative. Her mother and father were far from safe and the odds of her father surviving were slim. But she also knew what he would tell her if the roles were reversed. He hated the CPC and what they were doing to China and supported her in her activities with MI6.

Fred James interrupted to say that they were in position twenty-five miles from the platform, and it was time to launch the AUV. The drone overhead that was doing continuing monitoring had noted the landing of a helicopter earlier with three people emerging although they could not tell much about them as it was already dark, and they were hidden under an umbrella. But what only Dame Walters and Ming Lee knew what that her father had been implanted with a tracking device when she joined MI6. Dame Walters had known that Dr. Lee could well be a target. Ming Lee activated her app that showed the tracking and as she suspected one of those three was her father.

Ming Lee took Dame Walters aside and told her what the tracking showed. Neither were terribly surprised but were also pleased because there was a better chance of rescuing him on the platform than getting him out of mainland China. It was agreed that they would keep this to themselves for the moment.

The platform being in international waters outside of the Norway economic zone there was no legal authority for anyone to demand entry onto the platform even knowing they held a kidnap victim. Ming Lee also said to Dame Walters that perhaps her father would be able to find out what they are doing so his being on the platform could in the end be a blessing.

After further discussion it was decided there was no real reason to keep this information from everyone else on board and Ming Lee and Dame Walters called everyone to the dining room and brought them up to date.

"Ming Lee, I think it would be good if Nicos and I go to Oslo and get plans for the platform. They may have made modifications, but this was built in Norway and those plans could help us find your father when the time comes. I think that is probably all Nicos and I can offer right now." Maria and Nicos were excellent researchers and for now they seemed the best people to get this information.

It was agreed and shortly afterward the helicopter took off with Nicos and Maria. Craig went along as well wanting to coordinate with his office in Oslo. Dame Walters remained on board able to communicate from here with MI6 headquarters as she had installed on the ship the communications equipment she would need.

After long discussion of the problems they were facing Fred James and Harry got together with Captain Hastings to make sure that all their security procedures were in place and that the ship was prepared in case of an attack from the platform. While it seemed unlikely, they had been fooled twice now and were not wanting to be fooled again. Captain Hastings assured them that all their defenses were active.

Ming Lee, Harold and Meg got the AUV reach to launch. Again, they decided that they would actively maneuver the AUV and this time would take the risk of getting closer to the platform risking detection. Fortunately, they had recently built into the AUV with Kongsberg's help a night vision capability so that they could operate at night without having to turn on the lights that would give away their location.

Once launched it would take a couple of hours for the AUV to reach the platform. Meg agreed to man the controls up to the point of getting to the platform and letting Harold take over from there. Harold had added to the AUV a device that they would be installing on the metal base of the platform that would work as an acoustic device. While it was a crude listening device a second device was one that would be able to move onto the deck and perhaps give them both visual and audio capability.

It would be Ming Lee that would be operating these highly sophisticated devices that Meg had recently invented with the help of the British equivalent of the US DARPA (Defense Advanced Research Projects Agency) and which they hoped were undetectable. So tiny they were shaped in the form of a common fly. Capable of crawling or flying the only hope was someone did not bring a fly swatter on the platform.

Once in range Ming Lee released the "fly" which was working perfectly. Meg was watching over her shoulder to see how her newest toy was working. There were four of these on board the AUV but for the moment they were only launching the one. As it rose out of the water it flew on the deck and it had capability of switching from day to night views and infrared if needed. It could even make a buzzing sound if that were needed to add realism. Ming Lee was impressed and told Meg how great this was. Once they were satisfied it was working properly Ming Lee began a detailed look at the platform. Unfortunately for the moment the doors to the interior were closed so she could not get inside to look where her father might be being kept.

They were able to view the various pieces of equipment on the drill deck and those items did not appear to be your typical drilling equipment. The fly was sending back continuous video that was in turn being transmitted to both London and Langley for review and analysis. Hopefully, they could tell them what these items might be used for. Once they had seen all there was to see on the deck the fly was perched above one of the doorways and set to alert them when a door was opened. Perhaps they could gain entrance to the interior shortly. But for now, they had to wait. Ming Lee set her phone to alert her as soon as a door was opened letting her into the interior of the platform.

Chapter Ten

Craig was back in Oslo reading the paper the next morning and saw an article with a picture of Wang Po in Tromso with the Mayor smiling and holding up a Sister Cities banner. Banned in Sweden and other countries this was another form of soft propaganda intended to lull countries into believing China CPC was a benign organization interested only in free trade and good relations. Like the Confucius Institutes that served as propaganda arms for the CPC on college campuses and even in the K through 12 school system.

It reminded Craig of some of the early Nazi propaganda out of Germany in the 1930's. But he made note of Wang Po in the picture who appeared from the CIA reports he was overseeing the Nordic Prince and orchestrating whatever was happening on that platform. He was clearly a man to watch.

Back on Echo II a strategy session was underway with Dame Walters leading the discussion. "So far we have seen no new activity and it is interesting that the auroras are moving back north just a bit. My suspicion is that they are aware of our being in the area, and they have backed off their activities. But the fact they kidnapped Dr. Lee tells us that we have not seen an end to what they are doing."

"Have we any idea what is going on with the Nordic Prince?" Harry asked.

"Other than that, somehow they seem to be messing with the magnetic field, we still have no idea what they are doing or why. It seems to our scientists that they are at as great a risk as the rest of us but obviously the CPC thinks this will work to their advantage. I doubt it is because they want to increase tourism to see the lights in southern China." Dame Walters joked, but knew it was no joking matter.

"One thing we have noticed is that there has been a significant drain of electrical energy from Norway when these anomalies in the field have occurred. We think that Nordic Prince is responsible. So far it has not affected the electric grid in Norway but there are concerns in the government." Meg added what she had learned.

"I think we need to move Echo II back to Oslo and give all appearances we are satisfied with what we have seen on Nordic Prince. They have no idea we are aware the Dr. Lee is on the platform having tried to mislead us he is in China. In fact, the latest news out of China has an article that Dr. Lee is visiting his old university in Hong Kong with his picture hand in hand with old friends. Ming Lee tells me this is a picture from three years ago." Liz who had been doing research shows the picture around along with the news story hinting that Dr. Lee might return to his position in Hong Kong. It was a masterful, if disturbing, piece of disinformation.

Harold assured everyone that he and Ming Lee could continue to monitor the drone and the small fly camera on the platform even from Oslo. So far, they had yet to get inside but hoped that they would see an opening soon to move the small fly drone inside to see where Dr. Lee is quartered and perhaps hear conversations.

Back on the Nordic Prince Dr. Lee was being shown the work that they were doing. If he was there, he decided to make the best of the situation and learn as much as he could. Without overdoing it he was trying to show admiration for what they were attempting even indicating that he might like to be involved beyond the work on Nordic Prince. Wang Po was not fooled but he let Dr. Lee think that he might be. In fact, it was possible he thought that Dr. Lee might be helpful in ironing out some of the problems they had been having.

Dr. Lee still did not understand exactly what they were doing other than they were somehow manipulating the earth's magnetic field, but to what end was not clear. Nor was it clear how they were manipulating the field. Wang Po obviously did not trust him any more than he trusted Wang Po but perhaps he would need his expertise. He thought he had been kidnapped for his engineering expertise not realizing that he was in fact a hostage to prevent his daughter from interfering with the project.

As the Echo II made its way back to Oslo Ming Lee was at the controls of the overhead drone and the fly drone on Nordic Prince. She saw a crewmember open the door to the interior and quickly maneuvered the fly inside. She and Harold high fived over the success finally in getting into the interior.

Inside the Nordic Prince was a rabbit warren of corridors and rooms. And it appeared to have several levels. Ming Lee wished that Marie and Nicos had sent them the plans for the platform and she had Harold check to see if they had sent anything that would be helpful.

"Yes, they just sent this set of plans. It appears we are here on level 5." He pointed to an entrance door that led to the master control center.

"It looks like the top level is the control center and the next level down is the sleeping quarters, dining room, etc. The rest of the levels look like they are involved in the mechanical operation of the platform. Let us see if we can get to the next level down as that is likely where your father is located."

For the next two hours they spent time maneuvering the fly drone around level five but found there was a fire door between levels so they had to wait until one of the doors opened and then hope that the door on the next level would open. Frustrated they gave up when it was time for lunch. Ming Lee set the alarm so that if a door was opened they might get word in time to move through. She could do that from her phone though it was not as easy as working at the master control for the drones.

"It looks like there is a strong storm brewing that they tell us may last a couple of days. I hope that does not interfere with our signals for the drones. Fortunately, if so, the overhead drone will not be a problem as it can climb above the storm, but the fly drone will just park itself and turn off until we get back in control." Harold was reading the latest weather report that Captain Hastings handed him.

The forecast proved correct and when Ming Lee and Harold returned to the control room they found they no longer had control over the fly drone. It had parked itself on a ledge and shut down to conserve its power. While it could operate for some time it also needed to be recharged using sunlight at least once a day so conserving its power now was important. While they had more fly drones available should one fail without control over the drones there was nothing they could do now until the storm passed.

Outside, the seas were beginning to foam and waves were reaching ten feet. Captain Hastings slowed the Echo II and was carefully meeting the waves head on to avoid broaching. Stabilizers were working but that did not help on the up and down motion as the ship rode up and over the waves. It seemed they would be longer getting to Oslo than planned as meeting the waves not only slowed them, but they were zigzagging through the waves rather than on a direct course back to Oslo.

In the lounge Meg and Sally were conversing and speculating on what the Chinese were up to on the Nordic Prince.

"Meg, it seems likely that they have some idea how to manipulate the earth's magnetic waves but for the life of me I cannot see what advantage that is for them over the risk they are taking. Also, I have no idea how they are doing this." Sally was looking at books they had acquired on the subject but was finding no answers.

"Sally, we know they previously have tried to warm the polar ice cap to open the northwest passage over Canada for a shortened route to Europe and the east coast of the US. Also, that opens the door to mineral exploitation impossible now under the ice cap. While we stopped them the last time could that be what they are still attempting?"

"I guess it is possible but unlike the idea of using magma to heat the ice this seems an unlikely way of going about it but that said it is possible. If they can reduce the protection over the polar ice cap from solar radiation enough that could possibly be their objective. But if so, it is unbelievably reckless and dangerous."

Meg agreed but she also knew that they had been reckless in their past endeavors so taking risks was not beyond them. Still, it seemed they were missing something.

Just then the ship rolled sharply on its side as Captain Hastings misjudged the last wave that now had reached over twenty feet. He came on the speaker and apologized as Meg and Sally were collecting the books that had flown off the table as they rolled.

Picking up one of the books Sally stood frozen as she looked at the diagram in the book.

The book on electromagnetism and the early work of Tesla caught her attention.

"Meg look at this. I wonder if they are both trying to open up the Artic but also attempting to use the magnetic field to tap into the earth's electrical energy for an unlimited source of power."

Meg knew that Tesla had thought that he could provide free unlimited power transmitted wirelessly but never had the support or financing to complete his experiments and no one since had seriously tried to follow up on his ideas.

"While it seems the stuff of science fiction rather than science, I remember studying Coral Castle in Florida where giant blocks were somehow single handedly lifted to create a unique castle. And at one point as development drew near the man responsible even moved the entire structures to another location without any help. No one to this day has understood how it was done and some of the equipment left behind raises more questions than answer."

"More than a thousand tons of limestone was single handedly quarried and lifted into place and in some cases carved to create this unique place. It was created by a Latvian immigrant named Edward Leedskalnin who died in 1951 without revealing his secrets. Some think was simple leverage, others that it involved the secrets of how the pyramids were built and may have involved something called lay lines. But no one really knows."

"I remember he stood only 5 feet and weighed only 100 lbs. To think he accomplished this over 28 years is amazing. But what if he found a way to utilize the magnetic field to accomplish this result? We know that the Chinese have been visiting Coral Castle recently from what I was reading a while back."

Meg while doubting this was relevant was finding it worth exploring. She went to the computer and pulled up the website for Coral Castle. One of his friends debunks the idea of levitation and other alien theories saying his friend did this by hard work and ingenuity and he wrote a book "Mr. Can't is Dead! The story of the Coral Castle" in which he explains how it was done. Unfortunately, all we can see now is the cover as the book is out of print."

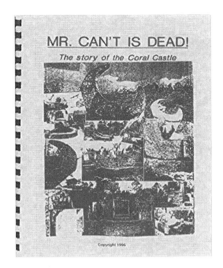

"That book is still available from the museum at the Coral Castle along with the original writings of Leedskalnin.   He claimed he knew the secret of how the pyramids were built and was fascinated by magnets and magnetism hinting that he was able to harness the energy to help build Coral Castle."

Meg and Sally pulled up the museum website and the list of books.   While thinking it unlikely there were leads here it was still   worth considering.   They noted there was   a   short monograph from 1945 on Magnetic Currents republished in 2013 with added title "The secret to Coral Castle"   but a quick review of the inside of the book online was not very revealing.

https://coralcastle.com/store/#!/Books/c/330
327

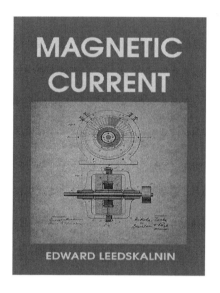

"While this is interesting, I suspect we will learn more from a less sensational and important work in the field, The 'Encyclopedia of Geomagnetism and Palomagnetism' and several copies of the book is waiting for us in Oslo as Maria managed to have several copies sent from Blackwell's in Oxford. A compilation of some 300 articles and 1000 plus pages on our subject."

"Just what I need some light bedtime reading!" Meg joked. But she also thought that it would be worth exploring to see if it has any clues on what is going on. They were grasping at straws, so any straw was worth grabbing at this point.

"I think we should divide up reading that book between you, Harold, Ming and I so we each have only 250 pages or so to go through. Then we can highlight any that seem relevant." Sally thought that a good idea and a way to speed up review of anything useful.

Chapter Eleven

While Ming Lee was increasingly concerned about her father, she knew that solving the mystery surrounding the Nordic Prince was perhaps her best chance of rescuing him as well as stopping what appears to be a dangerous experiment affecting the earth's magnetic field. She continued to monitor the fly drone which was still frustrated in finding a way into the lower level. And nothing could be done with it until that storm passed and they regained control.

It was Harold who came up with a solution for Ming Lee. He suggested that she have the drone fly into the ventilating system. It was powerful enough to work its way through the air currents and could travel through out the platform. But first they had to leave the platform and recharge the batteries which were running low. It would be tomorrow before they could try again to survey the platform. But on the way out they noticed a vent that would let them enter without having to wait for a door to open.

"Ming let's take a break from this. I wish we had left more than one fly on the platform but next trip we will do that." Harold knew that Ming Lee was increasingly anxious and that she needed to recharge herself as well as the fly drone. He suggested they go to the technology lab and work on the next fly drone as well as preparing for another visit to Nordic Prince. He knew this would take her mind off her father for a while. Not much of a break but it would be a diversion.

In the lab Meg was working on an update to the AUV. She was concerned that with the electrical energy being used on the platform that it might interfere with operation of the drones and the AUV.

"While they are quiet now from the readings on the electrical grid in the north of Norway it is obvious that the platform is draining enormous amounts of electrical power. That is not something any oil drilling platform would do. But just what they are doing is still a mystery." Meg was showing Harold and Ming Lee what she was doing to protect their equipment as well as that on the Echo II.

"What I am doing is trying to build a Faraday cage around all our electronic equipment. That is not a simple task with all the electronics we have on board as well as on the AUV and drones. But if successful it will protect these from a burst of electrical energy on the platform that might otherwise destroy this equipment or at the very least interfere with proper operation." Harold and Ming Lee were intrigued by what Meg was doing.

And it was working, Harold thought, to take Ming Lee's mind off her troubles. At least for now.

It was early morning when the Echo II docked again in Oslo. Nicos and Maria were waiting and had brought with them the books Maria had ordered from Blackwell's in Oxford. A good part of the morning was spent going over the papers in the book on geomagnetism looking for any ideas on what the Nordic Prince might be up to.

As of lunchtime they had failed to come up with any workable theories. But it did seem clear that the Chinese on Nordic Prince were somehow using electricity to interact with the earth's magnetic field and modifying it in ways they had yet to understand. It seemed that after a few days in Oslo they needed to return to Nordic Prince and attempt to discover its secrets. No one was more anxious to that than Ming Lee.

After lunch Harold and Ming Lee were once more at the controls of the fly drone which had successfully recharged and was good for another twenty-four hours.

Maneuvering the drone into the air intake on the platform Ming Lee was using the plans that Nicos and Maria had found and brought on board to fly the drone through the ventilating system to reach the fourth level where they suspected her father was being kept. It was not easy going as they were flying against the air currents from the blower, but the drone was up to the task. It took nearly an hour but finally they reached the vent on level four and could see the corridors and cabins to begin the search.

After two hours of maneuvering, they had success. In the lounge dining area Ming Lee saw her father sitting with Wang Po having tea and in a heated discussion. The audio was for some reason acting up and they could only hear bits and pieces of the conversation. From what they could tell Dr. Lee was telling Wang Po that their concept was flawed. That it was based on the ideas that Tesla had about the earth being filled with electricity that could be tapped at the surface providing unlimited and free energy. Wang Po was countering that they agreed but had found a better solution.

At this point the drone stopped working. Ming Lee feared that someone had spotted the fly and had used a fly swatter to destroy it. That was the only answer for why it was giving no signal. She was frustrated that they had not left more of the fly drones at the platform and for now further investigation would have to wait for them to send more via the surveillance drone and Ming Lee started the process of preparing another of the surveillance drones to act as a delivery vehicle for the remaining three fly drones they had on board. Fortunately, the surveillance drone could carry these to the platform although it would take most of the day for it to be ready to make the delivery. Meanwhile at least she knew that her father was safe. Knowing him she was sure he was working to derail whatever plans Wang Po had for Nordic Prince.

In the lounge Harry was meeting with Fred and Martin as well as his SAS operatives on board to see what plan they might make for getting Dr. Lee off the Nordic Prince. Dame Walters and Craig were sitting in as well.

"It seems to me our best chance of finding out what is happening on the Nordic Prince is to get Dr. Lee out. For some reason Wang Po seems to be including him in his discussions but Ming Lee tells me there is no way that Dr. Lee is cooperating voluntarily. He seems to be going along to find out what he can. And of course, for Ming Lee's sake we want him safely out."

"Security teams are already in place at their home in Australia though we doubt they will make a try for Mrs. Lee but then we did not think they would go after Dr. Lee either." Craig said disgustedly thinking they should have anticipated the kidnapping. But that was water over the dam.

"If we make a run at the Nordic Prince with Echo II or a helicopter assault, I worry for Dr. Lee's safety. It seems to me we need a stealthier plan" Harry nodded as Fred commented.

"What is the range of our two-person submarine?" Harry asked. Martin who had been working with Meg and Harold on it answered. "It has range of about 200 miles if you are making a round trip. Double that if you are going one way with a pickup by helicopter on the return."

"I think what we should do is to take Echo II from Oslo tomorrow and look like we are heading for Iceland. I am sure they are tracking us, and this might lull them into thinking we are satisfied and leaving. I doubt it but still seems worth a try. We can then launch the sub a bit closer to the Nordic Prince. Ming Lee should be alone on the mini sub and she is more than ready to do that. If she can get her father on board they can head back, and we will pick them up with the helicopter which is sling ready to pick up the sub if needed." Harry set out the plan and went around the room to see any objections or modifications. There were none.

"We need to talk to Ming Lee and see what she thinks." Dame Walters said as she called Ming Lee to join them.

Ming Lee was more than ready to follow the plan. She said that she would take with her the three fly drones and would launch them one by one as she got close to the Nordic Prince. She wanted to keep their battery life as active as possible. She relayed the fact that either the previous drone was destroyed or somehow malfunctioned. But she did not think if destroyed it would reveal much if anything. This was the problem with the fly drone. It so closely resembled a fly that it risked being swatted.

She and Harold had modified the fly drone so that they could land it on Dr. Lee's shoulder if possible and communicate with him to help with the rescue. Dr. Lee was aware of the fly drone as Ming Lee had told him about it so hopefully he would not think it was a common fly. Knowing Dr. Lee, he would understand.

The decision made, Fred called Captain Hastings and told him that this evening they would leave Oslo on a track taking them to Iceland. He wanted the ship traveling at its normal speed. While he doubted they would fool Wang Po it was the best they could do. Once they dropped the submarine, they might even change course heading to northern Scotland. That might convince Wang Po that they were leaving the area and he could safely resume his activities.

The rest of the day was spent getting the submarine and Ming Lee ready for the trip. Harold hated her going alone but there was only room for two in the submarine and she needed the extra seat for her father if she was successful. Ming Lee downloaded all the plans for Nordic Prince that Nicos and Maria had brought back and spent a good part of the evening studying them to see her best chance of extracting her father from the platform. It was not going to be easy. Her best hope was the ladder that led to the emergency exit module designed for any situation where the crew had to abandon the platform in an emergency. The good news was that it was not locked; the bad news was Dr. Lee would have to walk across the entire deck to get to it and she was not sure they would let him out on the deck. But all they could do now was try.

Chapter Twelve

On board Echo II that night all were on deck to watch the Northern Lights display only to find it was weaker than before and did not last as long. This seemed to fit with the fact that there was no activity on the Nordic Prince. Dame Walters suspected that this was due to their investigation and presence and that Wang Po was being careful to shut down operations temporarily. If that were the case, they had at least given the planet a breathing spell and time to stop any plan that would cause harm.

Dame Walters knew that if there were no danger, they would not have stopped the operation, nor would they have shanghaied Dr. Lee. She also knew their best hope now was to get Dr. Lee off the platform and find out what he knows. She had to hope Ming Lee was up to the task.

Back on the Nordic Prince Wang Po was on the phone to the ministry in Beijing that wanted to know his progress and when they could expect him to restart the operation. He pointed out that so long as Echo II was in the area he was stymied, but he hoped they would leave the area soon. Also, he was waiting for the last shipment of equipment from China that would allow them to intensify the effects and perhaps reach the critical mass that was important to success. That shipment was to arrive in the next couple of days.

Wang Po was disappointed that Dr. Lee was not willing to be more cooperative, but he felt he had ways to change his mind. Operations in Australia were not going as hoped as security for his wife had been increased. But Dr. Lee had friends in China and pressure could be brought to bear on them and their families if necessary. But for now, until the new equipment arrived there was no need to step up the pressure.

A storm appeared to be brewing that Wang Po was watching. It looked like for several days the storm would be in their area. This was perhaps good as it would make it difficult for Echo II to stand off the platform. He wanted them gone before the operation continued. He knew that Beijing was getting nervous and that was not good for him or his career. He was still fuming over the Petersons and Svenson and the stupidity of his men in killing them. That had to increase dramatically the interest of the British and Norwegians in what he was doing. But at least for now the damage seems to have been contained. He hoped.

That evening Wang Po invited Dr. Lee to dinner. Not that Dr. Lee had any choice. With him were the heads of the project and Wang Po wanted to see if Dr. Lee could be enticed to be helpful in solving some of the engineering problems they were encountering. He hoped that his innate curiosity would get the better of him and during dinner that seemed to be the case as Dr. Lee was engaging in the technical discussions. But Wang Po had warned his staff not to divulge more than was necessary as it was not time for Dr. Lee to find out the real activity on board. Instead, he was to be led down a different path. Wang Po was not stupid; he knew that a rescue attempt would be made and if successful he did not want Dr. Lee to be able to pass along sensitive information.

As the sun rose in Oslo Echo II was on its way out of the harbor. Captain Hastings had let everyone know of the increasing storm conditions. While he did not think it would present a problem launching the submarine he was concerned about the storm making it difficult if not impossible to recover the sub should Ming Lee be successful. As a result, he asked Dame Walters and Craig to see if there was a British or American submarine in the area that could rendezvous if necessary. Fortunately, the British submarine Falklands was in the area and the sub on board Echo II had the capability of attaching itself magnetically to another submarine if necessary.

The seas became rougher the further Echo II traveled toward Iceland. While Captain Hastings would have liked to change course to Scotland, he knew he could not do that until after the submarine was launched getting Ming Lee as close as possible to the Nordic Prince. He just hoped that the sea swell already at ten feet did not get much higher before it was time to launch.

One recent modification to Echo II was to create a moon pool from which the submarine could be launched. Below in the moon pool Ming Lee and Harold were getting the submarine ready to launch. Ming Lee was concerned that due to the weather she would not be able to launch the fly drone. If not, that would make the rescue even more difficult.

She was taking along uniforms like those that they observed on the crew of Nordic Prince along with a parka that would hide her features were it necessary for her to leave the sub and attempt a rescue on the platform. This was not the plan but considering the weather it was looking more and more likely that she would have to change the plan.

"Ming Lee you know what will happen if you are caught." Harold was more and more concerned as the plan looked like it was changing due to the weather. Risky before, that risk level had increased dramatically with the storm.

"Why can you not let Harry go or one of the SAS operatives?' Harold asked, but he knew the answer. There was no way Dr. Lee would trust anyone other than his daughter fearing that someone he did not know was simply a trick.

"Harold, I know the risk but you and I both know this is the only way." Ming Lee hugged Harold and she knew he was worried. If she admitted it, she was worried too. If caught her only hope was that they would use her as leverage on her father to get him to cooperate. That was bad but not as bad as other alternatives.

"You know if you have to go on the platform that their communication jamming will prevent you from reaching out to us?" Harold knew she was aware but was thinking out loud. They had been able to find a work around for the fly drone but not for cell phone or satellite phone communication. Even from the submarine once it was in the immediate area of the Nordic Prince.

"Harold you are worrying too much. I am well trained and capable of handling this. It is far less risky than when we were in the Pacific dealing with that EMP issue." Ming Lee knew this was different but the last thing she needed was for Harold to distract her with his concerns. Much as she appreciated his caring for her it was dangerous when it came to a mission. She had to be laser focused if she were to rescue her father.

It was only a few more hours before Echo II would be in position. Harold and Meg were going over the submarine and all the equipment that Ming Lee would be taking with her. It would be nearly dark when they would drop the submarine from the moon pool. Captain Hastings suggested that they not stop to unload in case the Chinese were observing. The sub could exit the moon pool under the ship and depart without anyone knowing.

When the time came Ming Lee quickly entered the sub checking all her equipment and instruments. With a final wave she was off and on her way. She estimated it would be three hours to reach Nordic Prince. She set the automatic controls with a stop notice when within half hour of the platform. After that she caught a few winks knowing that she would have be alert once she got close to the platform.

While the storm was picking up in intensity on the surface of the ocean underneath there was no indication of anything going on, so the sub was making a smooth passage. Echo II on the other hand had waiting two more hours before making a turn to the south and Scapa Flow where they would wait to hear from Ming Lee.

Captain Hasting and Harry had agreed that in case the Chinese were observing them they did not want to make the turn immediately after releasing the sub. Better to make them think that considering the storm they were heading for a safe harbor. Which was not far from the truth.

Harold was at the computer watching the movement of the sub and Meg was relieving him from time to time. They knew that Ming Lee would be using this time to get a little sleep, so they did not bother trying to communicate with her.

"I just hope the storm is not so bad that she cannot make contact with Dr. Lee using the fly drone, but it looks like she may have to board the platform. That will be tricky in this storm. I would not be surprised if she must wait. But knowing Ming Lee she will park the sub and use her scuba gear. I just hope if she does that that Dr. Lee knows how to scuba. There is no way the sub will be able to extract them from the surface in this storm." Harold was nervous and Meg realized it was his concern for his girlfriend speaking and not the scientist. But she did not blame him for being uneasy. She was as well.

"Harold just remember Ming Lee is not only Dr. Lee's daughter but she is a trained MI6 operative as well as an engineer. And the storm might in the end be a break. Everyone on the platform is likely battened down and with her parka and rain it is possible she can get around much of the platform without being noticed. Also, once inside she can find a safe place and release the fly drone to find her father and to let him know her plan." At least Meg hoped this was the case. As much as she wanted to reassure Harold she was equally concerned for Ming Lee.

Echo II was docking in Scapa Flow just as the submarine was an hour out from the platform. Dame Walters immediately left the ship for a meeting with Craig at the MI6 offices which were in the headquarters of the fleet stationed at Scapa Flow. Captain Hasting was telling John Peters the history of the base which had served the British Navy for as long as anyone could remember.

Martin Fredricks joined in the discussion having been stationed here just before his retirement. "The Vikings nearly a thousand years ago used the Orkney Islands Scapa Flow for their long ships. Seems appropriate we would be here now seeing answers for their modern ancestors. After WWI, the German navy was scuttled here and makes for interesting scuba diving not that we will have time for that on this trip. This was the chief naval base for the UK in World War I and II, but it was closed as a base in 1956. I was here only because we were working in support of your operation with Fred James." Martin brought out a chart book showing the location of the German battle fleet that served as a prime location for diving in the summer months.

Fred James joined them, and he too had been stationed at Scapa Flow for a time while in the Navy despite it being closed as a formal base. Since WWI he noted that the area had been used by the oil industry and remained a highly active port.

That evening on the deck of the Echo II they again saw the Northern Lights display which was as visible here as it was in Norway. Unfortunately, during the display the clouds from the storm front moved in and blocked the evening display.

"I wonder if Wang Po will use the storm as a cover for restarting the operation on the platform? It would be good cover as we cannot from the land at least see intensification of the display." John made a note to mention to Craig when he came back on board to have satellites and aircraft above the storm to check the status of the display in case there was intensification.

Craig later when John mentioned the possibility said he and Dame Walters had already started the process as they had the same thought as John about the Chinese using the storm as cover.

"I just hope the storm helps Ming Lee in her rescue attempt. Even more I hope she can bring back answers for us." Craig poured a scotch from the bottle he had brought back on board with him, and Fred, Marin and John joined in in a toast to Ming Lee wishing her luck.

Just at that time the alarm in the sub went off to tell Ming Lee she was half hour from the platform. She immediately began to get into her gear as she knew she would have to exit the sub and make her way onto the platform with the storm. She had brought along a dual mouthpiece for her scuba equipment and a double tank so that if she could find her father the two could make it back to the sub ok with scuba gear. Fortunately, Dr. Lee had at one time been into scuba diving and while it had been years, she was sure he could make it back with her. But first things first. She had to get on the platform undetected then find her father and after that, well, she just had to see. There was no way to make plans at this point.

Checking her equipment, she brought along two of the remaining three fly drones. Just in case she left the last on the Echo II and had Dame Walters planning for more to be brought on board Echo II if needed but that would take a few days. One final check and she was ready.

Taking off autopilot she was using her infrared display to position herself within one thousand feet of the platform. She did not want to move closer and risk setting off alarms even with her stealth equipment. She decided that she would rise to just below the surface to avoid their detection equipment as she swam to the platform. That would not be easy in the storm but if they detected anything it is likely they would attribute it to the storm. At least that was the hope.

It was not an easy swim in the storm-tossed waters. While deeper undersea the water was calm close to the surface it was not. Nor did she bring with her the propulsion system she normally would have used to ease the trip as that would almost certainly have set off the alarms. As a result, it was going to take her nearly an hour to reach the platform. Checking her dive watch she noted that she should reach the platform around two in the morning. Hopefully, any guards would be less than alert at that hour.

Chapter Thirteen

When Ming Lee reached the platform the waves were so strong she could barely reach and hang on to the escape ladder. It took her several tries, but she finally managed to hold on to the ladder and climb above the increasing waves. The platform seemed almost alive as the waves caused the platform to move and make grinding noises. It was much like design of a building to survive earthquakes or in this case to survive the pressure of water against the legs of the platform and its drilling apparatus.

As she made her way to the platform main deck she noted that the drilling rig, if that was what it was, had been raised to protect it against the storm. She suspected that the entire platform had been closed to protect it and just hoped there was not a lock on the door to the interior. While she brought equipment to overcome that doing so would surely give the alert to someone having boarded and that she wanted to avoid at all costs.

Ming Lee found a small equipment shed where she was able to get out of her diving gear which she hid out of sight under a tarp. She then put on the parka and a waterproof mask that she had seen people wearing on the platform. That she thought should protect her against identification and hopefully everyone was more concerned with the storm now. Checking to be sure she had the fly drones and her monitoring equipment she looked across the platform to the door to the interior. It would be 150 feet from the shed to the door and walking in the heavy wind and rain would be difficult. Fortunately, there was a guide wire on which she could hook a safety harness in case the wind blew her off her feet. She estimated the wind at over seventy-five miles an hour or the wind of a category 1 hurricane. And being the north Atlantic the rain was icy cold and stung as it penetrated any exposed skin.

Just as she was preparing to step out and hook onto the guy wire someone came out on deck and hooked on the other end. Looking around she found a place to hide herself as there was nowhere else for this person to go other than to the equipment shed. She found several boxes behind which to conceal herself.

It took nearly twenty minutes for the man to make it to the shed. She made note as she knew it would take her equally long the other direction.

She heard the radio crackle as he was speaking with someone inside the platform. "Next time you get to come out and get that damned equipment! This storm is getting worse. We cannot restart until this ends in any case so I don't know why they need this now." Ming Lee could understand the frustration and just hoped that what he was looking for was not in the box concealing her.

It took nearly half an hour opening boxes until the man found what he was after. Wrapping it in an oil skin pouch he carried strapped over his shoulder he spoke again into the radio saying he found the equipment they wanted and was heading back. The door flew open, and he cursed as it had flown back against the shed pulling his arm nearly out of his shoulder from what he was saying. Once more he had trouble closing the door but at least there was not a lock on it. Even if there was Ming Lee doubted he cared at this point or would have bothered to lock the door.

She waited a half hour before peering out of the doorway and saw the deck was clear. A look at her watch showed her it was now three thirty in the morning. She wanted to get inside the main structure well ahead of any change of personnel and before the day started. She just hoped no other piece of equipment was needed that would find herself meeting someone on the guy wire.

As she started out across the deck it seemed that the wind was gusting and perhaps even increasing. The stinging rain made her stop numerous times to turn her back to the rain. And it was taking her longer than the twenty minutes to make the crossing, but she finally made it to the door. Hesitating she knew this was a moment of truth. If there was a guard on the other side of the door then this was game over. But in for a penny she thought as she pulled open the door. Well, tried to pull it open. It seemed almost sealed shut with the wind and rain pounding against it. But finally, she managed to wedge it open a fraction. Enough for her to work her way inside.

There was no guard on the other side. Quickly remembering the layout of the Nordic Prince, she made her way to the stairs leading to level four. So far no one was around, and she made it quickly to the door to level four. A window let her check to see if anyone was on the other side. She heard talking and a group of four men walked by just as she was about to open the door.

Ming Lee breathed a sigh of relief that she had not just opened the door. While her parka and mask might hide her features, she felt sure most of those on the platform knew each other. At least with a parka on she did not have to worry about the identification tags everyone wore on their uniforms. While they had manufactured a fake tag for her, she had no doubt it would not protect her from scrutiny. The last thing she wanted.

She waited another five minutes before looking out the window again. This time the corridor was clear. Her objective was some fifty feet down this corridor to what appeared to be an equipment room that she doubted anyone entered absent a problem. She had considered a supply closet, but it was both too small and likely something someone would enter to get supplies. If so, there would be no where for her to hide. No, the equipment room was sizeable and looked as though it might have somewhere she could conceal herself if necessary.

She could hear the metal of the platform groaning under the onslaught of the storm. She knew this was by design, but it nevertheless was unnerving.

Back on Echo II, Harold was frustrated at the storm preventing him from using the overhead surveillance drone to track Ming Lee. He had hoped the infrared would let him spot her and then code the drone to track her as she moved on the platform. It was able to see her occasionally, but the storm was preventing it from performing normally. As expected, her communication gear was jammed on the platform and the storm was also making that impossible. Worried, he continued to monitor as best he could. Last he saw she had made it onto the platform and inside the main quarters area.

Ming Lee was preparing the fly drone for release and found an air vent in the equipment room that work allow it to fly through the HVAC system. She had located the quarters where her father was located so it was just a matter of flying the drone to his room and then hoping that he would awaken to let them discuss how best to rescue him.

It took her nearly an hour to reach the quarters as the air flow was causing her problems with the fly drone either bucking the air against it or moving too rapidly when air flow went the other direction.

Finally, she was able to see her father sleeping in his quarters. She let the fly land on the pillow near his ear and used the chirping to awaken him. She hoped he remembered about the fly drone and as he rolled over and spoke softly, she let out a breath in relief.

"Ming Lee is that you?" He said softly.

"Yes, father it is. I am on the Nordic Prince in an equipment room. I have scuba gear and a small submarine to take you off if we can do that and avoid detection."

"It will not be easy, but they have relaxed their guard on me of late. They had someone sleeping here in the room with me until yesterday but today I am alone."

"I have designed the fly drone where you can attach it to your collar, and we can continue to communicate as we figure out what to do." Ming Lee was pleased that the drone was working well and that the jamming was not preventing their talking. This would make the extraction easier she hoped."

"Father I suggest you get dressed and come to the equipment room. I will guide you once you are out of your quarters." This Ming Lee knew was just one tricky part of getting her father to Echo II.

Dr. Lee quickly dressed and as he opened the door, he found two crew members walking toward the break room.

"Could not sleep and need to use restroom." Dr. Lee announced hoping they would accept his excuse for being dressed this early in the morning. They nodded and went on their way.

It took only a few minutes for Dr. Lee to slip into the equipment room and hug his daughter. She had picked up another storm jacket and mask which he quickly donned and removing the fly drone which she then flew down the corridor to know when it was clear from them to leave.

Once outside and hooked on to the safety wire they found the storm had intensified even more. It was hard making their way to the shed where Ming Lee had stored her scuba gear. Dr. Lee fell several times as the wind gusted and even Ming Lee was having trouble staying upright.

Just as they reached the shed they heard alarm bells go off. No idea what the reason and could only hope they had nothing to do with finding Dr. Lee missing. Waiting several minutes Ming Lee saw no one exiting the main structure. She feared that they might begin a search and despite the storm any minute appear on the main outside deck.

"I think we have to risk going now. If they come on deck it is only matter of time before they find us." Ming Lee said quickly getting her father into the scuba gear and telling him what they would have to do.   She worried that the quarter mile swim to the sub would be too much for him but fortunately he was still in good shape using the gym at the university to work out as he had always done in his life. Good thing as this would be difficult especially sharing a mouthpiece.

The decent into the water went smoothly despite nearly losing their grip on the ladder to the emergency exit platform. One in the water they dove to a depth where it was calm and began to swim to the submarine. It took them nearly two hours to make the trip and by time they were inside both were exhausted, but happy.

Ming Lee quickly maneuvered the submarine away from the Nordic Prince and set the coordinates for meeting the British submarine that was hopefully waiting for them.

On the Echo II Harold was still frustrated that he could not see what was happening with Ming Lee and hopefully her father. But he was able to see that the submarine was moving and that was good news. He related this information to Martin who in turn was coordinating with the British submarine. It would not be long now, and they would know if Ming Lee was safe and had been successful.

Two more hours and Ming Lee saw the British submarine waiting. She sent a sonar ping which was returned. She was able to dock the submarine over the hatch and she and her father were able to exit into more comfortable quarters on the large nuclear submarine where the Captain was waiting to greet them.

"Captain thank you for being here for us. Are you able to communicate with Echo II?" Ming Lee wanted to let Harold know they were safe.

"Despite the storm we have no problem and once I saw you docking, I sent a message. We should have you back on Echo II in a few hours. Meantime how about some hot coffee?" Ming Lee and her father were more than happy to accept the invitation. The Captain was anxious to hear about the rescue and they spent a good part of the trip to Scapa Flow discussing how Ming Lee managed to pull off her rescue.

To try and fool Wang Po Ming Lee had had her father write a suicide note which he left in his cabin. It said that he refused to work with the project feeling it a danger to the earth and that he was going to jump from the platform to his death. To support the claim a piece of his clothing was torn and attached to one of the railings where he would be thought to have jumped. The fact the two crewmen saw him in the hallway at an early hour it was hoped would work to support the claim.

Dr. Lee doubted Wang Po would be fooled but he told his daughter that it did not matter. Wang Po needed an excuse to explain to Beijing how Dr. Lee escaped and to use the suicide was to his advantage whether he believed it or not. The lack of any of the alarms intended to alert the platform to intrusion would only help support the claim and the storm would account for the inability to find a body which would have surely been swept away if not sinking completely.

Chapter Fourteen

Several hours later the submarine entered Scapa Flow and docked next to Echo II where the mini sub was recovered, and Ming Lee and Dr. Lee were transferred to Echo II being welcomed with a celebratory party.

Dame Walters explained that they had sent word to Mrs. Lee of her husband's suicide but of course telling her it was not true but that she had to act as if it were. She even was to consult a solicitor to see what needed to be done to settle his probate estate. While it was doubted that Wang Po would believe the suicide the more real they could make it the better.

After the party began to wind down Dr. Lee and Ming Lee began to discuss what he knew about the Nordic Prince and what was going on that was causing a disturbance in the earth's magnetic field.

"I was only given pieces of what they are up to, but it seems they have bought into the idea of Nicholas Tesla who believed that he could generate unlimited energy from the earth and transmit that energy wirelessly much as he was able to do with messages before Marconi beat him to using wireless telegraphy."

"But Professor I thought that was debunked ages ago." Meg Roberts was taking the lead in asking Dr. Lee questions.

"True but there are still believers. After all we have people who believe aliens built the pyramids, crop circles exist from aliens or some natural phenomenon, lay lines that generate energy. There is Coral Castle in Florida and I could go on and on. But for every practical answer there is a dreamer who thinks it is possible. And after all, for eons people believed the earth was center of the universe, that the earth was flat, and every time this is disproven it only gives credence to those who believe in alchemy or in this case unlimited free energy transmitted wirelessly." Dr. Lee stopped sipping his tea as his throat was sore from the scuba trip to the mini sub.

"Are you talking about this?" Meg showed Dr. Lee a clipping from the 1904 New York American describing the Tesla Tower that J.P. Morgan started funding for Tesla in the early 1900's but was later abandoned and torn down in 1919. "Based I believe on his experiments in Colorado where he lit light bulbs wirelessly some 60 feet from his experimental tower and some claim he lit 200 plus at 23 miles but that was never proved."

New York American 22 May 1904

"That is the general idea and there is even a crowd funding site trying to raise money to rebuild the tower by a group out of Moscow, Russia. But so far they have managed to raise only a few thousand from gullible investors." Dr. Lee pointed out this was interesting since shortly after WWI Lenin approached Tesla thinking that wireless transmission of power should be something that the new Soviet Union should be involved in promoting. Tesla turned Lenin down saying he first wanted to prove his concept in the United States.

Dr. Lee pointed out that many believed people would never fly or go to the moon so sometimes the dreamers prevail. And the fact is that it is possible to transmit electricity wirelessly. Just not at low cost to generate or tap into the energy. And it is far from proven as practical

Dr. Lee punched in a search in the computer in front of him and showed everyone an article from August 2020 where a New Zealand start up that he had his students following was endeavoring to achieve long distance transmission of electricity. https://newatlas.com/energy/long-range-wireless-power-transmission-new-zealand-emrod/

He then pulled up the company website to show everyone what they were attempting. https://emrod.energy/

"The concept continues to intrigue scientists and businessman and who knows, one day we may actually see concrete results. At the same time remember when Tesla conducted his experiments in Colorado Springs, he put the entire city into darkness having pulled giant amounts of power from the grid that existed at the time. But what they are trying in New Zealand is transmitting already generated power."

Emrod claims the following:

- Emrod uses beams in the ISM (Industrial, Scientific, and Medical) band with frequencies commonly used in WiFi, Bluetooth, and RfID.

- Point-to-Point transmission means that power is beamed directly between two points. There is no radiation around the beam, as there is with high voltage wire transmission.
- Low power laser safety curtain ensures that the transmission beam immediately shuts down before any transient object (such as a bird or helicopter) can reach the main beam ensuring it never touches anything except clean air.
- Reduces electrocution risk associated with wires

And the major power distributor in New Zealand is an investor in the project.

"If this proves out it will result in incredible savings in construction and maintenance not to mention lack of wires. Ice storms will not shut the system down and there is according the Emrod no transmission outside the beam to raise questions of risk to humans or other animals. Not sure where birds will perch but that is another matter." Dr. Lee chuckled showing he was recovering from his ordeal.

"But this is transmission of power created by other means. What the Chinese are trying to do is to generate power from the earth's magnetic field and in doing so to reduce that field which they feel will melt parts of the northern and southern ice fields opening a trade route over Canada to Europe and the east coast of the United States without having to go through the Panama Canal. Also, it will uncover vast amounts of new mineral reserves."

"But Dr. Lee at what cost to the planet? Not only raising sea levels at risk from the change of the climate but increasing exposure to solar radiation." Meg was both fascinated but also horrified at what the Chinese were attempting.

"Yes, they did not buy into Tesla's idea that the earth was a giant battery from which electricity could be extracted but they do think that the magnetic field has potential for generating vast amounts of electricity. Even failing that the trade route and minerals uncovered by partially melting the ice caps have enormous potential." Dr. Lee stopped to let them think about this.

"But don't they also risk tipping the scale into a reversal of the poles with the increased danger that brings?" Ming Lee was engaging in the conversation now as well along with Harold.

"They do and as you know there are many who think we are in stage of such a reversal already and you are right this could tip us into such a reversal with unknown consequences. Some think that past extinction events have resulted when the poles reverse." Dr. Lee pulled up more websites on the computer that discussed the pole reversal. He pointed out the National Geographic article in particular discussing Alanna Mitchell's book on pole reversal.

https://www.nationalgeographic.com/science/article/earth-magnetic-field-flip-poles-spinning-magnet-alanna-mitchell

He also pulled up this item on the relationship of pole reversals to mass extinction events.

https://www.sciencenews.org/article/earth-magnetic-field-reversal-mass-extinctions-environment-crisis

"No one knows for sure if there is any relationship between pole reversal and mass damage to animal life but it certainly not something to mess with and that appears to be what the Chinese are doing." Dr. Lee paused before continuing.

"This study released in 2021 while far from conclusive is disturbing and perhaps even more disturbing is that the effects seemed to build far in advance of the reversal of the poles themselves as the magnetic field weakened." Waiting to see that everyone was still with him he added. "Note in the article on the study that they estimate the field at reversal was only 28% the strength of the field today but leading up to the reversal it was as low as 6 %. At those levels, the aurora events would be seen as far south as the equator. Not that anyone would be wise to be standing outside looking at them. There is even a theory that cave dwellers lived in caves to avoid exposure to the intensity of the sun." This article from Scientific American in 2019 is a good explanation." Again, he turned the computer so that everyone could see the article he pulled up.

https://www.scientificamerican.com/article/earths-magnetic-field-reversal-took-three-times-longer-than-thought/

"Then why do we not get governments involved to stop the Chinese from continuing with this experiment." Harry asked posing the question to Dame Walters and Craig Rathbone.

"Harry, I am afraid that the Chinese have managed to spread their propaganda to the extent that most countries fear to take them on. Add to that they have created a web of commercial ties both in terms of production and consumption within China that companies and governments fear challenging anything that China does. Look at their human rights violations and the abrogation of the treaty with Britain over Hong Kong, their stealing of technology, on and on. No, I am afraid that if we raise this with our governments or the United Nations we will get nowhere." Dame Walters looked at Craig for his comments.

"I think she is right. There is almost an incestuous relationship between China and other nations. They have enticed families of politicians to invest knowing that this gives them control and access. They have invested billions in various projects around the world to tie countries to their own fortunes. And in Covid they managed to hide from the world what happened, never letting WHO or other countries examine the origins until well after a year of the plague hitting the world and by then it was too late. And as the spread was starting, they were hoarding protective gear that they later sold at giant profits."

Craig paused before adding. "But other countries bear some blame too. NIH in the United States when 'gain of function' research was shut down because of the dangers it presented provided funding to the Wuhan lab to continue the research. Gain of function is hard to understand perhaps but what it did was to enhance a virus with the supposed concept of developing vaccines against new more virulent strains. But the risk it presented by virtually weaponizing a virus caused it to be stopped in the US and elsewhere. There are some who think this was the version that ended up being released in China as Covid."

"I am afraid Craig is right. Even if we could get governments involved by the time they decided to act I am afraid it would be too late. Damage may be irreversible. Could even be at this point and in any case, we have little time to act. And some governments might even support what the Chinese are doing. The Russians and perhaps some in Canada might support opening of the northwest passage not to mention opening up untold wealth in minerals. Greed and politics sadly can overcome science in many cases, as we have too often seen." Dr. Lee stated what everyone was probably already thinking.

"What about getting the press and social media focused on what they are doing bringing pressure on them to halt the experiment?" Nicos asked.

"Nicos I am afraid that the media and social media titans are all in league with the Chinese or with government officials who they support and will not embarrass. Unfortunately, media has become so highly politicized of late that honest journalism is a thing of the past. Most media today are nothing more than propaganda. While we might get a few independent outfits to focus I am afraid that by the time they generated enough interest it might well be too late." Craig commented.

"Professor, how far along do you think they are on Nordic Prince and do you think this is the only place they are attempting this?" Dame Walters asked.

"I got the impression that Nordic Prince is the only experimental platform from what Wang Po told me. What I learned on the platform is that they have managed some success in extracting energy from the magnetic field which is why you have seen the changes in the field and the movement of the auroras to the south."

Dr. Lee paused taking a sip of tea before continuing. "So far, they have not had a major effect on the field, but they are expecting new equipment any day that will magnify their efforts a hundred-fold, if not more. In essence they have created a giant electromagnet that shoots bolts of electricity far greater than any electrical storm into the liquid mass in the earth's mantle that is responsible for the creation of the magnetic field."

Dr. Lee continued, saying that "they also seem intrigued by the Tesla particle beam death ray that he proposed. While no one ever found evidence that he completed work there was serious interest from numerous governments. After his death, the FBI engaged President Trump's uncle, who was a scientist and electrical engineer, to go over all of Tesla's papers to be sure there was nothing that could affect national defense. He concluded at the time there was not. But Tesla's idea cropped up again during the Reagan presidency with the Star Wars project. In so many ways Tesla was influential far beyond his experiments and patents.

"I have no idea if they also have plans to augment the effects with some particle beam project but when I was on Nordic Prince I heard to engineers talking about the possibility. "

He was struggling to come up with an example to illustrate. "If I can use a poor analogy, consider a giant rubber band and you throw a basketball against that band. It then throws the ball back perhaps harder than your initial throw. Frankly, I doubt this is possible but what they expect and perhaps have achieved is that the energy returning is greater than that of the input. In that sense it is like what many nuclear fusion projects are attempting, releasing more energy than they put in. Again, he pulled up a couple of websites to illustrate.

https://spectrum.ieee.org/energy/nuclear/5-big-ideas-for-making-fusion-power-a-reality"

https://www.cbsnews.com/news/ten-serious-nuclear-fusion-projects-making-progress-around-the-world/

"From what Wang Po told me they also hope to use the technology in conjunction with a fusion power project with the energy created from the magnetic field to power a fusion reactor. But that is not what they are doing now. This is apparently only a first step for them." Dr. Lee again paused for any comments.

"But whether it works or not what the Chinese are doing is highly dangerous." Harry stated and Dr. Lee nodded.

"Dangerous to the magnetic field and if they manage to compress the time for the field to reverse then the effects on health and the polar ice caps will be enormous. This will make greenhouse gasses look like child's play." Harry noted and again Dr. Lee nodded.

"Then it appears we have our work cut out for us." Harry commented bringing the discussion to what steps they could consider.

"I suggest that we let Ming Lee, Harry and Meg spend some time with Dr. Lee and see if we can come up with a game plan for dealing with Nordic Prince." Dame Walters signaled for all but those four to leave the scientists to do their work.

Chapter Fifteen

Activity on the Nordic Prince was halted during the storm. The equipment that Wang Po was expecting had been delayed coming out of China and was not to arrive for another two weeks. Frustrated by the delay there was no choice but to give the crew time to rest and relax in Tromso. While the project was shut down it was clear that the magnetic field had regenerated itself and was returning to close to normal.

Newspapers in Oslo carried stories about tourists cancelling reservations due to the absence of Northern Lights to see that far south. The scientific community appeared less and less interested in the development now that things were returning to normal. They assumed this was simply some cycle of nature they did not fully understand. It would result in journal articles for some time to come trying to explain the reason for the anomaly.

In London Dame Walters was meeting with the Prime Minister to explain what was happening and trying to get his support for some action to stop the Chinese from restarting the project. While sympathetic he knew that he would face opposition even within his own party and this was not something he wanted brought up during the question period in the House of Commons. While he approved Dame Walters continuing to find a solution, he felt he was powerless to take any effective government action at the present time.

Craig Rathbone was finding the same resistance in the White House and Pentagon and he knew that many in the White House had financial interests in China with their family that he suspected would result in no action by the United States.

Back in Oxford Dr. Lee had joined with all those known as the Oxford group as he could not return to Australia until some solution was found. He and Ming Lee, Meg and Sally Fredricks were spending their days meeting with a variety of scientists to find a solution. So far without success.

Harry, Fred and Martin along with Nicos and Maria were researching military options but none of these seemed workable. True they could eliminate the Nordic Prince but so long as the Chinese thought the project viable, they would just find another platform and start over. While the delay could be useful committing an act of war was always dangerous. And getting government support was less and less likely.

John and Liz Peters returned to the classroom and their tutoring duties. They felt there was little they could add to the work the others were doing and thought it best to stay out of the way.

Evenings were spent at a dinner with all those involved getting together to report on progress, or in most cases lack of progress. Two weeks after their return from Scapa Flow they were having dinner at their favorite restaurant on the High Street in a dining room set aside for them. Dame Walters and Craig were present and had made sure the room was secure for discussions.

"We have ruled out any direct support from our governments although they realize the dangers involved but to risk a direct confrontation with China they are unwilling to consider. That also rules out a military option even a black operation. DARPA has been engaged as has their British equivalent but so far no ideas from those sources either." Craig summarized the situation.

"Even if we were to take out the Nordic Prince what we really need is a way to discredit the science, otherwise they will just keep trying." Dame Walters added.

"Our only advantage is that they seem to have bought Dr. Lee's suicide despite his looking rather well." Everyone chuckled including Dr. Lee.

"And with Echo II in Scapa Flow and all of us scattered they probably are feeling comfortable that we have abandoned any attempt to interfere with them. They are wrong of course but until we have an answer we are at an impasse. The only good news is that with the project having stopped for the time being the magnetic field has returned to its normal strength and so thus far they have not apparently done permanent damage." Harry added his thoughts to the conversation.

"We have started a bit of a scientific propaganda war of our own with DARPA and our scientists publishing articles both in the popular press, newspapers and some scientific journals debunking the ideas of using the magnetic field to generate wireless power and pointing out the dangers of interfering with the magnetic field. While it is unlikely this will stop the Chinese, it might have some effect in their scientific circles. At least that is the hope." Meg who had been working on this project laid out the steps they were taking to this end.

"Do we still have the overhead surveillance drone in place?" Fred James asked Meg.

"Yes, but the storm is continuing and looks like it will for a while, so we are not getting particularly good look at what is happening. We do know that much of the crew has been given time to go to Tromso for reset and only a skeleton crew is on board the Nordic Prince. That tells us they are not planning a restart of operations any time soon." Harold spoke up as he had been continuing to monitor the surveillance drone. "With the storm we have had to go to much higher altitudes to protect the drone and to recharge its batteries. That high it is practically useless for observation and with the cloud cover and storm even lower observation would not be useful."

Ming Lee had left one of the fly drones inside the platform but because of the storm the transmissions had been spotty and trying to maneuver it around impossible. Now it was resting on a shelf in Dr. Lee's old quarters which remained unoccupied now.

John and Liz Peters were continuing to work with the Viking Museum and its new interim director to see what could be done to get work started on the Viking 18 site. Loss of Jars was a real set back and it looked like it would be some time before work would get started again. John had set up a go fund me page for the project in Jar's name and it was gaining support. Hopefully in a few months John and Liz could take Jack and visit the site and get work started again.

Fred James and Martin were watching the storm which showed signs of easing. But behind it there was still a stronger storm that looked like it would be around Nordic Prince in another week. While that complicated any plans they might have it also hopefully was preventing any restart of the project while they sought answers to prevent that restart. So far no one had a good solution. A conference was scheduled for the next morning in the St. Edmunds dining hall which had been cleared and set aside for the meeting. It was hoped that some ideas and solutions would be presented then.

Chapter Sixteen

The next morning Ming Lee was sitting having tea with her father before everyone arrived for the meeting.

"We need to figure out what to do about bringing you back to life when this is over." Ming Lee was concerned how the CPC might react when it was known that Dr. Lee was alive and back in Australia.

"I have been thinking about that as well but do not have any good ideas, do you?"

"I think that perhaps we can claim that you were picked up out of the sea by a fishing vessel. Wang Po of course will not believe it, but it will give you and he both cover with the CPC. As for your being off Norway well we just must let that rest. CPC is aware why you were there and the cover story of your being in Hong Kong was just that. They can always claim you flew to Norway to help with the project and accidentally fell overboard. How does that sound?"

Dr. Lee smiled, thinking his daughter's time in MI6 had made her creative at story telling along with other things.

"Sounds believable and saves face for everyone involved which, as you know, is most important in China. Main thing is for them to leave your mother and I alone in Australia."

"I will get with Dame Walters and we will work out some kind of press statement for when the time comes. But I want to be prepared.

Dame Walters walked in at that point and they discussed with her what they had decided. She agreed with the plan and called her office to set the preparation of the release in motion to be ready when it was the right time. Craig was with her and he nodded his agreement.

"I think that is the best we can do, and it should cover the bases. My guess is that when this is over the CPC will want to cover this up quickly and this should help."

It took a while for everyone to assemble in the dining hall. Breakfast was set up buffet style with a full British breakfast which John and Craig had come to enjoy over the years.

Dame Walters called the meeting to order. She asked everyone's opinion around the table as to what ideas they had come up with presenting what she and Craig had learned. It was not much. While there were some ideas floated in the end none of them seemed to solve the really big problem. That was to make sure the project was not only stopped but never resurrected. The CPC had the resources to restart the program any time it wanted so the solution had to prevent that.

It was Ming Lee and Harold that in the end came up with the solution they could agree on. And why no one had thought of it before they wondered as it was a solution that should have come to them.

In their last adventure in the Pacific Ming Lee and Harold had use the EMP device that the Chinese had created to end that program. While normally an Electromagnetic Pulse resulted from a nuclear explosion that was not the only way to generate one. And the effects could be devastating as it could destroy any electronics that were not shielded. The tests they had done in Taiwan had shown that even military hardened equipment was destroyed which is why the Chinese abandoned the project and DARPA decided that it was too dangerous to consider working with. If you could not harden your own equipment against the EMP using it was just way too dangerous.

"But for our purpose here its unpredictability might be to our advantage. If we can use it where it operates to short circuit the electrical impulses on the Nordic Prince, the hope is we can make it appear that the project is unreliable and as with the EMP device itself they will stop the program. Best of all we can do this as we did in the Pacific from the overhead drone that is in stealth mode. They should have no idea what has happened or why."

"And as isolated as the Nordic Prince is there is nothing around it to be affected. Normally we would never consider using this but without any other solution this seems our best hope."

"We will have to wait to start the process just when they begin the operation again. We want to make it seem that their equipment caused the failure. Fortunately, we happen to have one of the devices here in Britain in mothballs." Ming Lee and Harold had been discussing this for the last few days and with no better solutions thought this just might work.

"Ming and I have been working on the device which Meg brought back to Oxford for us. We think we have designed it in such a way that it will not cause a total failure of the electrical equipment on the Nordic Prince immediately. We want it to appear that the equipment is malfunctioning, so they try and do a repair. Then at some point we will shut the entire rig down hoping they attribute it to the project. We will know if this has worked if they abandon the

Nordic Prince and hopefully sell it to one of the oil companies. Only then can we be sure they have given up." Harold seemed confident in the modifications they had made to the EMP device and Ming Lee let him take the lead in presenting the proposal.

"I have gone over the plan Ming Lee and Harold have developed and think this is clearly the best we can hope for absent any better ideas." Meg want to support the plan as she had already agreed it was likely the best that they could do.

Ming Lee then mentioned that she had left one of the fly drones on board the Nordic Prince and thought that with clear weather they should be able to use it to know when they were activating the electromagnet and monitor the effects of the EMP.

" If we are right that we have minimized the initial effects the fly drone should survive for the initial emissions. When we take the final step of full EMP as we know no hardening is known to exist to stop the effect so the fly drone will be useless. But we intend to recall the surveillance drone and add to it several fly drones that after the electronics on the platform are destroyed, we can send the fly back on board to know the reaction and how successful we have been to discourage further work." Meg had already started the process of recalling the surveillance drone having sent its sister drone to take its place temporarily. They wanted Echo II to be no where near the Nordic Prince when this action was taken. In fact, it was departing Scapa Flow and heading for Portsmouth to arrive this evening.

"I think we should all go back on-board Echo II tomorrow and cruise to Cannes for a holiday. I have bought out all the apartments in the building with ours so there is plenty of room and ample security. That will throw off any suspicion of our having been involved. And we can control the EMP and drones from Echo II no matter where it is located. With the weather set to improve in a week my guess is this will be the time we need to act." Fred and Angelique were happy to offer both Echo II and their Cannes apartments for this deception as they had planned this trip earlier and put it off when the Norway issue arose.

Going around the table one last time Dame Walters found all agreed with the plan. Meg was given the authority to proceed with the drones and Ming Lee and Harold were tasked with working with the EMP device. The biggest problem of course was there was no way to test the lower effects of the device. But Dr. Lee had reviewed the work Ming Lee and Harold had done and approved. He thought it should work as they anticipated.

It was a little longer than they originally thought before all was ready. Meg had repurposed the surveillance drone to carry the EMP device along with four more of the fly drones which were protected from the EMP device being above its lens that pointed directly at the Nordic Prince. Harold and Ming Lee had worked on the communication devices to control all the drones and all seemed to be working perfectly.

The weather was beginning to ease, and the surveillance drone had noted that the crew had retuned to the Nordic Prince and that a delivery had been made of crates which they assumed contained the new equipment they had been waiting for. It was time for Echo II to head south to the Mediterranean.

When all were on board and the Echo II was passing Gibraltar, Meg announced that they were beginning to see activity on the Nordic Prince, and it appeared they were restarting the electromagnet. Dr. Lee had said that it would take a full twenty-four hours to reach full charge ready to discharge into the mantle. It was decided that the first EMP event would take place twelve hours into the process and would be at the lowest setting.

Harold had his fingers crossed that he and Meg and Ming Lee had made the proper modifications and that the EMP would not be at full power on its first use. It was important that it only interrupt the main electromagnet if possible, with minor other effects. The inability to test the EMP modification worried him but he was hoping for the best.

That evening was a noticeably quiet dinner as everyone was on pins and needles wondering if the EMP would work as planned later that night. While they were enjoying the warmth of the Mediterranean as they approached Cannes they were all uneasy knowing this was the critical time.

At the twelve-hour mark all assembled in the control room of the drones. Ming Lee wanted Harold to be the one to activate the EMP and Meg had agreed. Ming Lee had moved the fly drone into position in the Nordic Prince control room hiding it in the ventilation shaft but able to hear what was being said and observing reactions.

The electromagnet was clearly building up its power when the EMP caused it to completely malfunction. While lights dimmed and there were probably other effects so far it was working as planned. Ming Lee could hear consternation in the control room as they sought to find the reason for the malfunction. Wang Po was called and stormed into the room.

It was hours later, and they had apparently made replacements to the damaged gear and were starting up the electromagnet again. Once more they were giving it twelve hours before activating the EMP. This time Ming Lee moved the fly drone back away from the control room as the plan was to up the power of the EMP.

This time the EMP device not only caused the electromagnet to cease working but it caused damage to other electronics on board. But again, it was not a full discharge of the EMP.

The fly drone back in position it was able to learn that no one had any explanation as to why this was happening. Speculation that somehow it was creating an EMP of its own causing damage beyond the electromagnet. New computer equipment was ordered from Tromso along with other items that needed to be replaced.

While most of those on Echo II had moved to the apartments in Fred and Angelique's building in Cannes Meg, Harry, Ming Lee, Dr. Lee and Harold stayed on board to monitor conversations on Nordic Prince and be prepared to do one final burst of EMP when the time was right. It was decided that they had to probably do two more low level EMP to convince them that there was something wrong with the design of the project.

They needed them to become so frustrated that they were prepared to abandon the effort.

Ming Lee moved the fly drone to Wang Po's quarters so she could overhear his conversations with Beijing. She was pleased with what she was hearing. It seemed there were some in Beijing that had not agreed with the project to begin with, and they were using the failures to date to urge cancellation of the project in its entirety. Wang Po prevailed on continuing to try and find the flaw and fix the problem. Beijing gave him a week after which if he had not solved the problem he was to return to China with his crew.

It was three days later after two minor EMP bursts that it was decided it was time for the coup de grace. At least they hoped this would be the last straw for those on Nordic Prince. This time they would allow the electromagnet to charge for eighteen hours making them think they had solved the problem. When the time arrived, Harold insisted that Dr. Lee be the one to initiate the final EMP burst. He did so and it was quickly apparently that all the equipment on the Nordic Prince had been destroyed. Ming Lee flew one of the new fly drones back to the platform to overhear the conversations. What they heard was confirmation that this had indeed done the trick. Wang Po had finally given up when his scientists said that obviously the electromagnet had caused major failures throughout the platform.

It took several days for a resupply boat coming to the Nordic Prince for the crew to be able to abandon the rig. With no communications they had to wait for the ship to come to evacuate. Another storm was brewing to the north and the crew was taken off just in time. A celebration was in order in Cannes tonight and Fred and Angelique were making the arrangements.

It was decided to wait a week for Wang Po and the crew to be back in China before the press release was issued announcing the rescue of Dr. Lee from the north sea.

The press office had done a remarkable job of saying that while he was recovered some time ago that he had been ill and the fishing vessel had continued its fishing rather than return to port while Dr. Lee had been in a coma for much of the time and had only recently recovered his memory when the fishing vessel returned to its home port in Reykjavik, Iceland. He was expected to be hospitalized for at least a week before being able to return to Australia.

In Conclusion

The trip to Cannes had been a wonderful break for everyone and Dr. Lee managed to do his recovery on the beech and seemed to be enjoying himself as much as everyone else. Ming Lee was pleased that he seemed to be getting along well with Harold and approved of their relationship. She just hoped her mother would agree.

Fred and Angelique had arranged for a private beach that adjoined their apartment complex which was easy to do now that they owned the entire apartment. They made sure everyone knew they were welcome to use the apartments any time that they wanted and that included Dr. and Mrs. Lee.

While the ladies shopped the men enjoyed sitting in the local restaurants at outside tables and a glass of Pastis. They were also getting used to the French idea of a leisurely two-hour lunch. Indeed, it would be hard to get back to cold, rainy Oxford next week.

"I hear that Wang Po has disappeared in China." Harry commented. Dame Walters and Craig had been keeping the ears of MI6 and the CIA to the ground and found that the powers that be in China were not at all happy with Wang Po. Those that opposed his project from the start were using its failure to make sure he never could try again, It seemed that the plan had worked to discredit the program.

As for the Nordic Prince an oil company out of Norway made the low bid for the platform and instead of making use of it planned to tow it to Scotland where it would be scrapped.

The only downside was the return of the Northern Lights to the north of Norway. No longer were they seen nightly in Oslo. But the tourist traffic to Tromso had increased dramatically as a result as it remained one of the best places to see the remarkable display. John and Liz were looking forward to summer there helping to restart the Viking 18 project. Nicos and Maria along with Harry and Meg planned to go along taking the children with them this time.

It seemed things were going back to normal for the Oxford group. But then you never knew what adventure may once more involve the talents of this unique group of friends.

Epilogue

I hope you enjoyed this latest adventure of the Peters and their friends. If so, I hope you will consider posting a review on Amazon. As an author these are deeply appreciated. If on the other hand you did not enjoy this book Amazon offers a generous refund policy. In any case I thank you for spending your time to read Scandinavian Secrets and hope you look forward to the next books in the series.

This is a work of fiction but some of the science mentioned is real. The fact is that the earth's magnetic field has been weakening in recent decades making some scientists think that a polar inversion is perhaps underway. Probably not in our lifetime as these events take considerable time. The book mentioned earlier is worth reading on the history of the poles switching and how our magnetic field works to protect us from what would otherwise be devastating solar radiation. You can find that book on Amazon.

The Spinning Magnet: The Electromagnetic Force That Created the Modern World--and Could Destroy It
https://www.amazon.com/gp/product/110198516X

/ref=ppx_yo_dt_b_asin_title_o03_s00?ie=UTF8&
psc=1

Google "polar reversal" and you will find a lot of articles on the internet discussing the subject. The same is true of Coral Castle in Florida for those interested in this strange and still mostly unexplained creation. Coral Castle is indeed real. https://coralcastle.com/

The city of Tromso is real but the Viking 18 site is from my imagination as is the Nordic Prince drilling platform. The Kongsberg Marine AUV HUGIN is quite real and an amazing device. It is worth a trip to their website to see how this operates. https://www.kongsberg.com/maritime/products/marine-robotics/autonomous-underwater-vehicles/AUV-hugin/

The Chinese Confucius Institutes and Sister Cities programs are real. Unfortunate because they tend to be propaganda arms of the CPC promoting positive views of China while ignoring the many human rights abuses the CPC would prefer remain hidden. As for the story line here of course, that is pure fiction. So far as I know there is no device to tamper with the magnetic field, at least I hope not! While drones exist of course the capabilities attributed to the ones here are again fiction as is the oceanographic vessel Echo II.

While for purposes of the story the ideas of Tesla for unlimited energy are adopted these ideas were disproved many years ago as knowledge of the earth and its magnetic field grew and were better understood. Still, it makes for an interesting idea for the novel. For those wanting to delve into Tesla and his inventions (his invention of AC current is still in use today of course) consider this book written by the Chair of the Engineering department at Princeton. Tesla: Inventor of the Electrical Age which you can find on Amazon at this link:

https://smile.amazon.com/gp/product/0691057761/ ref=ox_sc_saved_title_1?smid=A34BTUVE1794N 8&psc=1

For those who have not read the first books in this series the first book, Operation Black Amphora, and the second book, The Devil's Dagger, and the third book, Treasures of the Deep, as well as the fourth book, Mystery on the Mekong, all are available on Amazon thorough my author page at www.amazon.com/author/scottro along with other of my books. In addition, recently hardback as well as paperback and e book editions are available for purchase.

Alas despite the best efforts at editing and proofreading errors are still likely to creep into a manuscript and those errors are mine alone. I apologize for any that you might find and will hope to correct in future editions.

Wishing you many years of reading enjoyment and my thanks for spending time to read this book and hopefully all five in the series to date. A sixth in the series, Tragedy in Tenerife, is currently underway and hope for release in the near future. A sample is included below for those who cannot wait!

Robert Scott April 2021

Tragedy in Tenerife

Chapter One

It was raining a cold rain as John Peters walked across the commons of St. Edmunds Hall, a small college and part of Oxford University. His umbrella and rain jacket were hardly keeping the rain off as the wind was slanting the rain. He was headed for the college pub, a small. warm and inviting refuge for such a bleak day. Meeting his wife, Lady Liz Armstrong Peters he was looking forward to spending time discussing their plans for the holidays.

Giving Liz a peck on the cheek he slid into the well-worn dark mahogany seat and ordered a pint of bitters.

"Tell me what Fred and Angelique James have planned for us?" John asked.

"They have Echo II provisioned for a month in warm waters of the south Atlantic this year. A visit to the Canary Islands with stops on the way along the Spanish and Portuguese coast. Madeira and the Azores too."

"That sounds just what we need but can we take Jack along?" Jack was their young six-year-old son and he loved spending time on Echo II oceanographic vessel owned by Fred James and used as much for his personal yacht as for its oceanographic capabilities although those were formidable. Fred and his wife Angelique lived part of the year in Oxford working with John and Liz with their archaeological institute and with Harry and Meg Roberts in their SAS Security Services. All were good friends and had spent many years together on a variety of adventures.

"Fred says Angelique would be heartbroken if the children were not on the cruise. They anticipate this time will be nothing but a pleasure cruise." John thanked the server as his bitters arrived at the table. He had a hard time initially getting used to warm beer but with the cold snap just before Christmas it hit the spot.

"What about Randy and Athena?" Randy and Athena were the same age as Jack and children of Harry and Meg Roberts and Nicos and Maria Andreas, respectively. All three children were in school together and close friends as were their parents."

"Yes, looks like all three will be there although Nicos and Maria will join us in the Canary Islands as they want to spend time with her father in Mexico City and her mother in London. Nicos also wants to spend part of the holidays with his parents in Crete and they have not seen Athena now in over a year." Meg was pleased to see that things were working out for Nicos and Maria.

"I assume that Martin and Sally Fredricks will be with us too?" They were close friends of the James and lived in Oxford now. Fred and Martin have been friends since their Navy days together and after Martin retired a few years back he too had joined what was known as the Oxford group with Sally, along with John and Liz, teaching at St. Edmunds and Martin working with Fred mostly with SAS with Harry and Meg.

"Yes, and of course Ming Lee and Harold who are just back from their honeymoon in Fiji and having spent time with her parents in Australia." Ming Lee and Harold had finally taken the leap into marriage a month ago and it had been a fun celebration in the chapel of one of the colleges big enough to accommodate all the well-wishers. Dame Walters, M of MI6 and Clark Rathbone, director of the CIA were there along with all their friends. Over the years through a series of adventures they had become close with the Oxford group and considered family. Ming Lee had asked Dame Walters to be her maid of honor and Harold had asked Clark as his best man. They felt this was the best way not to slight any of their other friends and Dame Walters and Clark had been pleased to be asked.

"What about school for the kids?" John asked.

"Not a problem, Sally has agreed along with Angelique to tutor the kids and their school has agreed to let them work remotely for the time school is back in term." Liz thought that it would be wonderful for all of them to share this month in the sun together."

"Well, I don't know about you, but I am ready to get out of this cloudy, rainy cold weather although with snow in forecast we might just have a white Christmas this year." John signaled the bartender for another bitters, but Liz declined. It was not quite time to tell him that she was pregnant again and not drinking. When she declined John gave her a puzzled look and then realized what this meant.

"You have something to tell me?" John smiled as Liz smiled back.

"Yes, I was waiting as it is very early, but it looks like Jack will have a brother or sister this summer." Liz was pleased to see John's happy reaction to the news. They wanted at least two or three children and there was never a right time, but right or not it looked like they would be adding to the family shortly.

"Don't tell me Meg and Maria are also pregnant?" John joked. "It would not surprise me but no, I do not know if they are."

After an hour in the pub John and Liz decided despite the rain, which was easing, to walk down the High street toward Carfax towers and do a bit of Christmas shopping. Liz had already set up for them to meet Meg at the café on the corner for an early dinner and then the girls would be off shopping.

At dinner, the friends were clearly excited at the prospect of a month in the sun together on the Echo II. The girls already planning how they would spend their time on the islands and the guys deciding on some scuba diving. All were looking forward to a break from the winter weather in Oxford. Little did they know this would not be the pleasure cruise everyone was planning.

Made in the USA
Middletown, DE
01 November 2022

13889380R00110